Falling for the Lawman

Kirkwood Lake Romances
Book 1

Ruth Logan
Herne

DEDICATION

To Robyn and Kim, two women who weren't afraid to be farm women. What beautiful examples you've set for me! God knew what He was doing when he introduced me to the two of you! I hope you love Piper's story... because this gutsy gal reminds me of both of you!

CHAPTER ONE

"TO EVERYTHING THERE IS A season, and a time for every purpose under the heavens."

Raised in the pews of a sweet country church, New York State Trooper Zach Harrison embraced the poetic lines of Ecclesiastes one hundred percent.

But it couldn't and shouldn't apply to constantly crowing roosters.

He refused to look at the dashboard temperature readout as he climbed out of his car. The trickle of sweat along his neck proved the meteorologists correct. Low nineties by noon, even here in the hills of Western New York.

He shut the driver's door and ignored the initial blast of mid-July heat. The best thing about working nights to help cover summer vacations was the cooler temperatures. The worst? Trying to sleep in the middle of the day in a new house, with his father pacing in the next room, the sun beating on the roof, no central air and the neighbor's rooster crowing on the quarter hour.

He couldn't change anything too major about the house. Not yet, anyway. The down payment, closing costs and lumber to replace the rotting backyard deck put a serious dent in his savings.

Three weeks ago his summer had stretched before him,

filled with work on the force and his new home. One phone call had changed all that.

"Are you a *real* policeman?"

Zach turned, surprised, and a small part of his heart went soft in the space of a beat.

Identical twin girls peered up at him from behind an aged catalpa tree. The twins were petite perfection, mirror images of each other. Pink and purple pigtail ribbons danced in the July wind, a breeze that did nothing to soften the hot, humid conditions. "Yes." He stooped low, knowing his size could intimidate, captivated by this unexpected pair of miniature greeters at the nearby farm. "I'm Trooper Zach."

"I'm Dorrie." The first girl beamed him a smile, open and broad, tiny white teeth a contrast to her latte skin beneath the purple pigtail ties. "And this is my sister, Sonya. We're five."

"Nice to meet you." Zach put out his hand and fought a wince as a rooster crowed again, the loud reason behind his late-morning call on his new neighbor. New chicken dishes filled his brain. Maybe something deep-fried for the bird that aggravated his father and interrupted Zach's midday attempts to sleep.

"Are you getting ice cream?" Dorrie wondered. She pointed to the line at the window of a converted barn. "Aunt Piper has the best ice cream anywhere."

"Grandma helps," interjected Sonya, obviously determined to give credit where due. She looked like her more assertive sister, but one finger twirled the pink ribbon tied around her left pigtail, the anxious action speaking louder than words.

"But not Uncle Chas," Dorrie added, determined to keep the record straight. "He hates this place. So does our mom. Uncle Colin, too."

"Doralia! Sonya! Where are you?"

Zach straightened, remembering his task, and it wasn't

to fall in love with two kids who would cause their father plenty of worry once they turned into teenagers. "They're here."

A robust woman of similar coloring strode his way. She nodded thanks to him, then gave the girls an earful in a mix of English and Spanish with a hint of what might have been Native American thrown in for good measure. The girls dropped their chins, pretending penitence, but Zach knew they'd disappear again in an instant, given the chance.

That was the one thing he'd loved about being raised on a farm in Central New York. Freedom, once his work was done. Time to roam. Study nature. Hunt white-tailed deer come fall. Find birds of all sorts, tucked into nature's God-given homes. But it was the *only* thing he'd liked. The endless hours of farm work, day after day, dawn to dusk, confronting the weather, market prices and wind-borne disease?

Not so much. He liked his steady law enforcement paycheck, a promised pension, clear expectations and visible rewards. Bad guys got put away. Good guys stayed safe. It was a tangible world with measurable results, which suited him.

The girls hustled into the country-themed barn. Zach followed. His eyes took a moment to adjust to the change in lighting, but when they did, he was surprised.

The other buildings showed wear and tear no doubt caused by lack of money or time. Probably both. The Southern Tier of Western New York had fallen on hard times over a generation ago. Businesses closed, factories shut down, employment dropped to all-time lows.

But this barn glistened. Bright white coolers were located to his right, their glass doors immaculate despite the throng of people and busy hands. Inside the coolers, glass bottles formed military-straight lines. He moved closer, intrigued. Intrigue gave way to surprise as he read the labels. Whole milk…2 percent milk…skimmed milk…egg nog…

Eggnog? In midsummer? Either these folks lived by a different calendar or they were way ahead of the game prepping for Christmas.

The rooster crowed again, the pitch and length of his practiced voice taunting Zach. Clearly the bird didn't realize Zach packed heat in the form of a lightweight Glock.

The twins buzzed past him, back toward the door, dragging a small brown-and-white goat between them. The creature needed a haircut, which reminded Zach he could use one himself. But the sight of them bound for fun touched a wistfulness inside him. Their presence instilled a warmth he didn't know existed five minutes ago.

"May I help you?"

He turned.

His heart melted. It was an absurd reaction because he'd met a lot of pretty girls in his life, but the one watching him now, with more than a hint of question and a bite of sass in her gaze, could have been cast in a country music video. Her trim T-shirt read: "Yes, I'm the farmer. How can I help you?" A faded Kirkwood Lake Central School ball cap was pulled down properly on her forehead, while a long reddish-brown ponytail swung from the hat's opening. Thin jeans, faded and worn, said she wasn't afraid to work for a living, and farm boots gave testament to the shirt's claim. A pair of work gloves poked haphazardly from her right hip pocket. Right-handed, then, most likely.

"Zach Harrison. I live…"

"Piper McKinney." She stuck out her hand, then paused and withdrew it. "Oops, forgot. Cops don't like to shake hands. My bad."

She was right, but how did she know that? Some cops

were fanatic about not shaking hands for various reasons. Zach wasn't one of them. He'd been on the force for eleven years, and he'd defused many situations with a simple handshake. In this case? Shaking this particular hand couldn't be called a hardship.

He extended his hand. She waited two breaths, maybe three, then inhaled and touched her fingers to his. He gripped them gently, noting the work-worn surface of her skin.

"Piper?" A voice, ripe with question, interrupted the moment.

She withdrew her hand and turned. "Lucia. This is Trooper Harrison. He lives…?" She raised a brow again and made a face. "I have no idea where he lives because I never gave him the chance to say so. Sorry, Officer. This is my stepmother, Lucia McKinney."

Zach nodded politely. A hint of distrust marked the older woman's eyes. She swept his uniform a furtive glance, as if she'd had less-than-happy run-ins with police before. That would be something to think about later. "Nice to meet you, Mrs. McKinney."

"Lucia is fine," she told him. Her voice, a touch gruff, sounded work-worn. Zach understood that. Farms were life-draining occupations. He'd seen that firsthand, hence the pledge to work somewhere else. A pledge he'd kept from the day he graduated from the academy.

Lucia turned her attention toward Piper. She jutted her chin toward the back. "Chas is grumbling about the new pasteurizer."

"Of course he is." Piper offered a bright smile that stopped short of her eyes. The resignation in her gaze made Zach want to have a word or two with Chas…. Whoever he was.

Her expression called to the protector in him. And while this woman's straight-on gaze said she needed little protection, something in her stature said otherwise.

Piper shifted her focus to Lucia. "Are the girls still in the back room or did they escape again?"

Zach waved toward the door. "That way. With a goat."

"Ach, those girls!" Lucia flapped her apron in Zach's general direction, as if it was his fault the two miscreants had performed another vanishing act. The college-age girl behind the counter took care of the next milk customer while Zach shifted his attention back to Piper.

Her expression defined the current chaos as normal. Zach wasn't sure if that was good or bad, especially where kids were involved, but he remembered some early escapades from his youth on the family farm. And he'd survived.

"Are you here on a case?" Piper interrupted his musings.

"No."

"Have we done something wrong? Maybe you need milk. Or eggs. Unless you're waiting for Ada Sammler's daily baking of bread? It should be arriving any minute."

He had no idea who Ada Sammler was, and while fresh bread sounded great, he wasn't about to store bread that would go moldy in days because his busy schedule meant he wasn't around often enough to eat it. Even with his father there. Dad wasn't eating all that much. Another source of concern.

He simply wanted peace and quiet. The sooner the better. "It's the rooster," he said again. "Roosters," he repeated, stressing the plural.

She frowned, not understanding, and waved to a young family as they strode through the doors, then again to an aging couple. "Albert, don't think for a minute I'm letting you haul jugs of milk to the car on your own," she scolded, but her grin took the sting out of the reprimand. "You hang on to Edna so we don't have another broken hip on the prayer roster and we'll handle the bags, okay?"

The old man smiled, and the peaceful look on his aged face made Zach wish that kind of contentment for his father. But they'd have to find a way to redistribute a wagonload of Marty Harrison's anger and Zach had no clue how to do that. *You there, God? I'm open to suggestions these days. Not nearly as stubborn as I used to be. If you've got any bits of wisdom to throw my way, I'm ready for them.*

Piper pulled her attention back to him and smiled as if what he had to say mattered. The smile almost made him forget his request, she was that engaging. Bright-green eyes sparkled beneath thick brows, and her classic athletic look said she stayed in shape to do her job, not just to look good in a dress. Though Zach was pretty sure she'd look great in a dress.

Another rooster crow brought him back on track. "Him. Them." Zach waved a hand to the right. "I bought the house around the corner on Watkins Ridge, and I need the roosters to quiet down during the day when I'm sleeping."

She stared at him, then tried to hide a grin by coughing into her hand. "You want quiet roosters? There's a novelty."

"I've been working nights…"

"Close your windows."

Brilliant idea, except for the extreme summer temperatures. "Too hot," he shot back.

"Get a fan. Install air-conditioning."

"A room air conditioner blocks sound. That's not safe. And I've got hot-water baseboard heat, so installing central air would be crazy expensive."

She tapped a finger to her jaw, contemplating him. "Let me get this straight. You want the roosters to be quiet because you can hear them, but you don't want to install a room air conditioner to block the noise of the roosters because then you *can't* hear things. Right?"

Okay, it sounded preposterous put that way, but essentially, yes. He wanted to be able to hear a home invader, so the idea of a noisy air-cooling unit wasn't on his list. But he didn't want to hear annoying birds that refused to respect his backwards sleeping habits. "Kind of."

She threw him a bright smile that said "conversation over" and started to back away. "I've got a cutting of hay to bale and get pulled in before this afternoon's possible thunderstorm, so Zach—" she raised her index finger to her cap and tipped the brim in a gesture of respect "—I'm going to take what you said seriously right after I get in acres of forage, oversee the afternoon milking and pray this drought doesn't ruin an entire year's corn crop or I'll be feeding cows with nonexistent funds. I'll be doing that while keeping two little girls alive although they seem determined to tempt fate, running a busy dairy store, and keeping a neat and tidy farmhouse. I may or may not be lying about that last one." She turned and strode away, but not without one more parting shot. "Sleep well."

Grudging respect rivaled frustration for his sleep-deprived emotions. He *had* sounded somewhat absurd, and she wasn't afraid to call him on it. And the teasing grin she sent over her shoulder as she walked away was a look that said she'd be looking forward to "round two."

That was enough to make him eager, too. Right until the roosters let loose again, reminding him that in nine short hours he'd be back at work. He'd really like to spend half a dozen of that sleeping.

Piper dragged herself into the house just before nine that night. Lucia rose from a side chair as Piper slipped through the back screen door. She bustled to the kitchen, a fast-moving woman despite her wide girth. "You go wash. I'll warm supper."

"I can handle it, Luce. Sit down. Relax. You work every bit as hard as I do. I don't need you to wait on me."

"I'm older and bossier," the middle-aged woman shot back. "Therefore I give orders in the house. You give them on the farm." She lifted her shoulders in a gesture of agreement. "And we share bossing people in the store and the dairy. It works, no?"

"It does."

Piper climbed the creaky stairs. The thought of fresh-smelling cotton pajamas called to her, but first she peeked at the girls.

Dorrie and Sonya shared one bed despite efforts to separate them. With no father in their lives, and their mother's abandonment nearly three years ago, the girls clung to each other. They would enter kindergarten this fall, in separate classrooms, and Piper and Lucia had wrestled with that decision for weeks.

Was it right to split them up? Would it instigate more trauma? Could they handle being apart?

Piper had no idea, and the published experts disagreed, so she and Lucia followed their common sense and decided separate classrooms were in the girls' best interests. But neither woman pretended the girls would embrace the concept. They'd shared a Sunday school class the past two years. But pricey preschools didn't fit the farm budget and Piper's schedule left little time for playdates, which made the girls more dependent on each other. With their first semester of school approaching, Piper wished she'd given the girls more play time with other children. That would have prepared them better for September.

"You made soup?" The scent of spiced beef greeted Piper as she descended the stairs fifteen minutes later. She met Lucia's matter-of-fact gaze with a smile. "In this heat?"

"Crock-Pot." Lucia nodded toward the cooling bowl on the table. "And one of Ada's loaves from yesterday, toasted. I turned the rest into croutons for selling."

"You're a marvel, Lucia."

The older woman shrugged. "Waste not, want not. The hay is in?"

"The front fields, yes, and good quality. It's dry, though, and that might make our second cutting nonexistent. The lower field of alfalfa gave a great first yield, but the lack of rain is worrisome. The girls managed to stay alive, I see."

Lucia's expression soured. "What one doesn't think of, the other does. And so beautiful, those smiles…they flash them as they plan one more way to turn my hair gray. Bah!" She raised a hand of dismissal as she changed the subject. "You cannot worry about the weather. Your father never learned this lesson. His daughter should." Lucia sent her a stern look tempered with love. "God is, was and ever will be. Weather is not of our doing. So we deal with it as it comes, no worries, because people of faith do not worry about what they cannot control. But this problem." She hooked a blunt thumb north and her gaze narrowed. "The policeman. He will make trouble, no?"

"Because of the roosters?" Piper scoffed at the idea, then shrugged. She'd cringed every time she made a tractor pass along the hay field that day because either Raven or Starlight seemed determined to crow along the fence that bordered the trooper's backyard. "I advised him to block the noise. He was less than appreciative. So yes, he might make trouble. And I get his point, Luce, about sleeping, but really?" She made a face of disbelief that drew the other woman's nod of agreement. "Don't move to the country if you can't handle the country."

"I can handle the country."

Piper turned, chagrined.

Lucia straightened. Alarm darkened her features.

Six feet of square-jawed good looks stood beneath the porch light at the back screen door, dressed in uniform. Piper clapped a hand to her mouth. "Oops."

"But there's no reason to have those birds outside my back door, crowing at each other all day," Zach continued. Raising a hand, he waved light-seeking bugs away from his rugged, handsome face. "You're not raising chicks, you're selling eggs, and you don't need a rooster to do that. What use are they on this farm, Miss McKinney?"

Piper stood and faced him, then waved him in. "We're neighbors. Don't stand on the porch, swatting bugs. Come in. And call me Piper. Want coffee?"

"You have coffee on? It's almost nine-thirty."

She nodded to her one-cup brewing system. "Twenty-four/seven. I don't have the patience to wait in the mornings. This is easy. And perfect."

"Then, yes. I'd love a cup. And a rooster muzzle to go with it."

She laughed. Even when serious, he was funny, and she liked that in a man. Guys who could laugh at themselves? That kind of man was rare in her experience.

Regardless, she was keeping her birds, no matter how cute the trooper was in his gray serge uniform with a freshly shaved face and somewhat sleepy eyes.

Guilt mounted, but only a little. The girls loved the roosters—they'd raised them right out of the egg—and no way was she parting with them. Dorrie and Sonya had enough on their plates. The roosters stayed. End of discussion.

"So. About the birds…"

"Cream? Sugar?" She held out both in matching stoneware after she handed him a mug of fresh, hot coffee. "This is real cream, straight from the dairy. Unless you'd prefer milk?"

"I love cream in my coffee." He sat, raised the little pitcher in big, broad hands and handled it with a dexterity Piper appreciated. "And sugar. And I have to sleep sometime, right?"

He stared right at her, letting those blue eyes sparkle

with charm, their brilliance tempting her to smile back. But she'd dealt with irksome neighbors in the past. These days it was a common farmers' lament, as if running a weather-dependent business wasn't work enough. No, today's farmer had to deal with keeping the neighbors happy and dealing with calls from the town officials listing a litany of complaints.

Folks wanted fresh food but not the work, noise and odor that came with farming. Her father had caved now and again.

Piper wouldn't. She'd already put heart and soul into saving this place. Give an inch and folks wanted a mile. Not on her watch. And avoiding Zach's flirty look was easier when she remembered how good Hunter had been with those long, intent gazes.

She'd been young then. She felt plenty old now, with her father gone, the farm to run, kids to watch and her brothers haranguing her on a regular basis. "There must be some way to block the noise. Or switch shifts. You could work days," she suggested.

Lucia coughed a sound of warning. Cops made her nervous. The twins' mother had gone to jail as a teen, and that never sat right with Lucia. Going toe-to-toe with a trooper who now happened to live next door would worry her.

"We're shorthanded at the moment, so my schedule varies," Zach explained. "Days. Nights. Afternoons." He shrugged. "It will be like that for a while. That's a long stretch to work on no sleep."

He was being nice. Not demanding. Simply stating his case, and that made Piper more willing to compromise. For the moment. "I'll put the boys in the far pen tomorrow. On separate sides, or they'll fight. But I can't put them in the hutch in these temperatures. They're heat-sensitive."

"Me, too." Zach stood, smiling. Upright, his presence

filled the room. His height, the broad shoulders, the uniform that made him stand out in a crowd…

He stood out here, too. Piper rose and followed him to the door. He glanced at his watch. "I expect you need some sleep yourself. Milking comes early."

Did he know that from personal experience, she wondered?

"It does." Piper offered her hand, glad she'd gotten cleaned up as soon as she came in. Although why she should care was something to examine later. Much later. "Let me know how tomorrow goes. If having the roosters in the barn pen helps."

"I will." He tipped his gaze down, his expression warm. Grateful. A little teasing.

She didn't want to smile back. Hold his attention. But she did, and for long, pointed seconds neither one breathed, caught in the moment, her hand melded with his.

Lucia coughed again.

The sound brought Piper back to reality. He might be the nicest guy in the world, but she'd learned her lesson. Cops were in her "high risk" category, and flirting with a neighbor?

If things went bad, you still lived next door. No way could the situation end well.

She extricated her hand, stepped back and pasted a small, polite smile into place. "Have a good night."

He swept her outfit a quick glance and a grin. "You too."

Tired and surprised by his unexpected visit, she'd forgotten the faded Scooby-Doo pajama pants and matching t-shirt.

Great. She looked like a twelve-year-old. And her hair was half-wet, half-dry, a bedraggled mess.

She shut the door and turned.

Lucia rose from the recliner in the adjoining living room. She shot a dark look toward the door as Zach's engine rumbled to life outside. "You want trouble again? Another broken heart?"

"Luce—"

Lucia's firm gaze stopped Piper's argument. "I know I am not your mother."

She spoke the truth. Piper's mother had divorced her father when Piper was still in grade school. She'd moved away with a massive share of the heritage farm in her pocket, a share that put the farm in the red from that day forward. She'd never looked back.

Her father married Luce months later, his quick remarriage inciting plenty of small-town talk. He adopted Rainey as a child, bringing the beautiful girl into the fold. But when Rainey went on her wild-child sprees as a teen, tongues wagged faster. Chas and Colin were in college by then, but Piper had been here, helping hold down the fort. It hadn't been easy.

"We have had our differences," Luce acknowledged. "But that does not change my love for you. You had your heart broken once by an officer. And I had mine broken when they took my daughter to jail."

"Luce, you can't blame the police for what Rainey did." The last thing Piper wanted to do was hurt Luce's feelings, but where Rainey was concerned, Luce's judgment proved faulty. "She broke the law. But she paid her price, and who knows?" Piper closed the space between them and embraced the older woman. "Maybe she's clean now. Maybe she's gotten her act together and she'll come back, ready to be part of the family again."

Luce didn't return the hug. She stood stiff and straight, fighting emotion. "And what do we do if this happens? Trust her? Welcome her? Hand the girls over as if it is okay to leave your babies for years?" Eyes wet, she stepped back. "I don't know what to wish for. My daughter to return? Or my daughter to stay away and leave those babies in peace?"

Piper understood the dilemma. Rainey's teenage antics had resulted in prison time. She'd straightened herself out and started her associate's degree in prison. She'd stayed squeaky-clean, no drinking, no smoking, no drugs, obeying her parole. She'd gone to church and sang with them, her beautiful voice soaring on the words of ageless hymns.

Then something had pushed the headstrong girl beyond her limits. She got pregnant, had the twins, then disappeared before the girls' second birthday, leaving only a short note.

They'd heard nothing since. Three years of not knowing. Was she alive? Safe? Straight? Or had she fallen back into the vicious cycle that claimed her teen years?

Piper kept it simple. "We pray. God's bigger and stronger than any force on earth. We pray for her and for the girls. And us."

Luce nodded, fighting emotion. "All right." She dashed an apron to her eyes and moved toward the kitchen. "If you and Berto need help in the morning, call me."

She said that same thing every night, because she didn't trust Piper's brother to show up. Chas hated the farm.

He despised being in the fields, so she put him in charge of the milk production room, where fresh, ultra-pasteurized dairy products were bottled for sale under cool conditions while she labored in the hot sun. He had two people working with him, and still whined about it all, the narrow profit margins, the uselessness of tempting people with vintage-style glass bottles of fresh milk products.

Piper knew that thin profit margins beat zero-profit margins. She bit her tongue on a regular basis, not wanting to fight with her older brothers.

She loved the farm.

They didn't.

But they couldn't sell without her permission. Unless she went under. And no way was she about to let that happen.

CHAPTER TWO

"MISSING SOMETHING?"

Zach's questioning voice rumbled, ripe with wry humor.

Piper forced herself to maintain an outer calm she didn't feel and looked up from a tractor seal that seemed determined to give her a hard time. She saw Zach holding the girls' Nigerian dwarf goat, a favored pet. The brown and white miniature creature looked quite content in the big man's arms. "Beansy? Where did you find him?"

"In what used to be my vegetable garden."

First the roosters. Now the goat. Piper winced until she read the humor in Zach's eyes. "You haven't lived there long enough to have a vegetable garden."

"It appears he didn't know that. How'd he get out?"

"The better question is, where are the twins? And did they engineer his escape or escape right along with him?" She jumped down from the huge wheel and strode toward the barn door as she spoke, using the sides of her jeans as grease rags. Thin streaks of motor oil left telltale marks. "He was in your yard? And before you answer that, why aren't you sleeping? It's after twelve. Too hot? Or did the roosters wake you? Because I penned them and I haven't heard them crowing, but I can block the sound. Was it them? They woke you?"

"My current dilemma is which question to answer

first," he drawled, his slow talk making a valid point. She tended to jabber in stream-of-consciousness fashion. Maybe she'd slow down someday when she didn't have to cram thirty hours of work into a twenty-four-hour day.

"Yes, he was in the yard," Zach continued. "My father noticed him. And I did catch a quick nap, but something's come up. I'm taking the next couple of weeks off, so I didn't need to get more than that today."

"You'll be ruing that choice tonight," Piper supposed over her shoulder. "Dorrie! Sonya? Where are you?"

Silence answered. She reached into her pocket and withdrew her cell phone. When Lucia answered, she put out an APB on the girls.

"Berto's got them," Lucia assured her. "He's giving them a ride on the hay wagon before lunch. Why? What have they done now?"

Piper wasn't sure they'd done anything, but from the look on Zach's face, she figured the two girls may or may not have been trying to catch a glimpse of their new favorite policeman.

He'd been in uniform both times she saw him yesterday. Tall. Broad. Strong. Dark hair. Bright blue eyes that warmed with humor.

Today?

Better, if possible. He wore a short-sleeved T-shirt that proclaimed him the winner in last year's October breast cancer run, along with well-worn blue jeans. Piper noted his pants with a glance. "Jeans? In this weather?"

"I'm a farm kid," he admitted, which surprised her because she'd noted reluctance in his gaze as he scanned the farm the day before. "You always wear jeans on a farm."

"True." She slipped the phone back into her pocket and turned toward the barn, noting the fresh oil streaks on her work pants with a grimace. "Denim's handy when you forget to grab a stack of rags while doing engine maintenance. Luce will have something to say about this, no doubt."

Her look of repentance made him smile. "Where would you like Beansy?"

She growled and led Zach and the goat through an adjacent barn. Calf pens lined the semi-shaded side of the building. One pen sat to the side. The perimeter fencing was decked out with trinkets and miniature signs done in little-kid scrawl. 'Beansy the Goat' read one. 'Beware of Goat!' said another. A half dozen similar signs swung strategically around the enclosure, leaving no doubt about the ownership. "Here we go, Beans. Scoot in there, and bleat real loud if they take you out again." Piper scratched the little fellow's head and Zach was pretty sure the tiny creature preened.

"Beans is a pet, I take it."

Piper hemmed and hawed, then nodded. "I'm a softie and I have a hard time saying no to those girls. A tendency I get to rue every single day."

Zach couldn't help but laugh. "Who wouldn't? They're the cutest things I've ever seen. So Beansy is theirs?"

"Beansy was left behind by folks who moved away and abandoned their animals. Luke Campbell brought him by last spring."

Luke Campbell was a deputy sheriff for the county. But did Luke's visit here mean he and Piper had something going? And why should Zach care if they did? One glance her way said he had a grocery list of reasons to back away from this attraction, but the look on her face made him wish the list away. "But Beansy is just a baby."

Piper shook her head. "He's not. He's a small breed, and he's smaller yet because he wasn't properly fed, but he's probably two years old. Luke thought the girls would love him. And he was right. We have room. And forage. And he's itsy-bitsy adorable so that's a plus." Her voice went soft. Sweet. Maternal. But one snap of her hand to her thigh brought back the dogged farmer within the pretty, petite woman. And Zach had enough of farms and farmers growing up to last a lifetime. "I've got to get back to that oil leak. Zach, I appreciate what you did." She tipped her hat and held up her grease-stained hands as evidence. "I'd shake your hand but that's pretty undesirable right now, so I'll just thank you again for Beansy's safe return."

Despite the sheen of grease on her palms, Zach didn't find her hands one bit unbecoming, but he shoved that opinion into his "don't go there" file. "You're welcome." He started walking away, but something—manners, interest, guilt—made him turn back. "Do you need help, Piper? I know a few things about tractors."

She turned and met his look. For long seconds they stood separated by a matter of ten feet, but the look in her eyes said they might as well be light-years apart. "You're kind, but no. I'm fine."

Cool. Concise. As if she were shouldering him off because she loved working with smelly, greasy engines?

No.

Because she didn't want to work on the engine with him.

Zach reached into Beansy's enclosure, gave the fuzzy fellow a nice ear rub, then headed toward his house. Helping on a farm ranked dead last on his list, so most of him was glad she'd rejected his offer. But he'd glimpsed the tired, frustrated look in her eyes when she first turned his way in the barn. And it had deepened when she'd been unsure of the girls' whereabouts.

A part of him longed to ease that frustration, but he'd grown up witnessing that look on his father's face. It wasn't a game he never wanted to play again.

"You didn't need to take time off." Marty Harrison poured a cup of coffee, gaze down, grinding the words that evening. "I *don't* need a babysitter."

"Dad, I—"

"And I *don't* need someone hovering over me twenty-four/seven. What I need is…" Marty stared out at the fields beyond, the adjacent dairy farm a reminder of all he'd lost due to medical error, a mistake that had triggered a bunch of wrong decisions. Decisions made by Zach.

His father's grim expression increased Zach's guilt. "I didn't take the time off because of you, precisely. I realized that if I'm going to get that deck done out back, I'd better do it before summer ends. I thought I might be able to enlist your help with it. If you want to, that is."

"Keep the old man busy?" Bitterness deepened his father's already cryptic tone. "That way I won't get into any trouble?"

Easing Marty back into a semblance of normalcy was going to be harder than he expected, Zach realized. His father's flat gaze deepened Zach's concern, but other than good old-fashioned time, how could he help Marty's mental and physical recovery? "We could drive down to the lake," Zach suggested. "Or take a walk."

"A walk to nothing is still nothing."

Zach knew that wasn't true. He'd often walked on his own as a kid. He continued the habit now, as an adult. Quiet walking time cleared his head. Eased his mind. The measured pace allowed him to be at peace. Notice the birds, the winged creatures chronically busy but generally unworried.

In a job that dealt with the seamier side of humanity too often, walking soothed him. If Marty Harrison wasn't walking *to* something, to be *somewhere*, the walk wouldn't make sense. But things were different now, and—

Marty's shoulders squared. His jaw softened. He held the coffee cup higher. Tighter.

The sound of children laughing drifted across the evening air. A host of them, from what Zach could hear. Another shout of laughter had Zach noting the time. Almost eight o'clock. That must mean ice cream at the dairy store. He moved to the back door and swung it wide. "Dad, come on. Let's go get some ice cream."

"I'm not walking down to the lake for ice cream." His father's ludicrous look said Zach was crazy and annoying. "It's nearly a mile."

"Come on." Zach pointed southeast and gave his father a lazy smile. "I've got a surprise for you."

Marty's face darkened. His eyes looked down for several beats, but Zach had outwaited tougher guys than his father lots of times. He stood, patient and persevering, allowing his father time to take that first step forward. Shouts of childish laughter tempted Marty outside. By the time they skirted the near pasture and worked their way around the closest barn, the sight of children laughing, playing and shrieking paused Marty's step.

"What are they doing here?" he asked.

"Ice cream after the game." Zach pointed toward the dairy store tucked on the protected side of the barn they'd just rounded. "Just like you did with us when we were kids."

Not exactly. His father hadn't been a mainstay at soccer games or Friday night football. On a farm there was always something to do, fix or tend. Running kids to games had fallen to his mother.

That brought to mind Piper that afternoon, hanging over the tractor, trying to put big, heavy things right when she should have been spraying crops or turning cut hay. Guilt speared him for not taking the time to help. He knew farm equipment. And his size made tractor parts a whole lot easier to handle, although she'd probably jab him in the solar plexus if he suggested such a thing. And she'd done all right on her own to this point, so why was he torturing himself about it?

Kids of all ages dashed here and there. Some sported baseball attire. Others were dressed in soccer gear. Parents sat or stood in small circles across the wide yard, watching the antics with small-town comfort. "I wonder if they've got Parkerhouse cherry?"

Marty's hopeful expression made Zach wince inside. Whatever this cherry thing was, he was pretty sure the inviting ice cream window was about to disappoint his father. Frankly, Zach wasn't sure how many more downturns his father could handle, which is exactly why he'd taken emergency leave for the next couple of weeks. Maybe just having Zach around would help Marty through the worst of this adjustment period.

The short lines moved quickly. Lights would light up the parking area after awhile, while the scattered picnic tables set beneath sprawling farmyard trees hugged cooler shadows. When they got to the front of the line, Zach was surprised to see Piper, Lucia and the same college girl he'd seen yesterday all inside the window. "You work here at night?"

The sound of his voice got her attention, and unless Zach had lost his policing skills in the twelve hours he'd been off duty, she looked happy to see him. Excited, even.

Which made two of them.

Her smile inspired his, but he felt a moment of abject fear when Lucia asked, "What can we get for you, gentlemen?" Zach dreaded the thought of Marty's disappointment over something as simple as ice cream.

"You got Parkerhouse?"

Lucia's quiet frown said they didn't. Zach was ready to point out the long list of flavors they did have, but Piper's voice interrupted him. "Sir, do you like amaretto-based Parkerhouse or vanilla?"

Marty's eyes lit up. "The almond stuff."

She threw him a smile, winked and scooped a generous serving onto a cold stone set off to her left. Taking a tong's worth of cherries with just a little juice, she worked the ice cream between two flat paddles for about thirty seconds. She arched a glance back toward Marty. "Did you say cone or dish?"

"I didn't," he replied, the more appreciative tone in his voice making Zach breathe easier. "A cone," he decided. "One of those." He pointed to the waffle cones and Piper's smile said she approved.

"These waffle cones are the best," she told him as she plied the ice cream mix into the cone. "In my humble opinion…"

Lucia's cough said Piper's opinions might not be as humble as she made out. Her timing deepened Marty's smile, which then eased some of Zach's concern.

"…the cone makes the treat," Piper declared. She sent Marty an arch look. "Too soft, too sweet, too well-done." She shrugged narrow shoulders clad in a T-shirt beneath the ice cream apron. "The best ice cream deserves a solid cone."

"I concur." Marty took a taste of the cone she handed him. She watched, waiting, clearly hoping she'd pleased him, and in that moment Zach discovered more to like about her. Patience, in an impatient world. Concern, as if Marty's satisfaction mattered. And a hinted joy as if she loved the task at hand, taking care of business after working in hot fields and barns all day.

"Delicious. And an almost perfect balance of cherries to ice cream. A couple extra cherries would always be welcome." Marty smiled at her and Zach was pretty sure that was the first genuine smile he'd seen since bringing his father home post-surgery five days before, even though the smile was accompanied by veiled criticism with the word "almost."

Zach had lived with those "almosts" for a long time. Almost smart enough, almost good enough, almost strong enough…

But Piper just laughed out loud. "You come back tomorrow or whenever and I'll add more, okay? Although the secret to a perfect Parkerhouse cherry ice cream?" She shortened the distance between them by leaning out the window. Marty bent closer. "Is to make the palate long for that next bite of fruit. Too much and the texture is messed up. It's all about ratio, but you come back," she repeated, "and I'll use more cherries. Deal?"

"Deal." Marty confirmed the pact with a brisk nod.

"Zach. What can I get for you?" She turned her attention his way while Lucia and the girl handled two other customers.

"Vanilla."

She almost burst out laughing, but held it in, with effort. "You're serious? That's it? With thirty-one flavors at your disposal?"

"I'm very serious about my ice cream, Piper. Why taint a perfect blend with nonessential additives?"

"Oh, brother." Skeptical, she made a face, reached for a cone, then paused. "Clearly I'm forgetting myself when you're around. Or maybe your adorable father has me flustered. Cone or dish?"

Adorable? Marty Harrison? Industrious, ambitious, driven, forceful, yes, Zach reasoned mentally.

But nothing about the hard-core farmer could be labeled adorable. Could it? "First, I like that I fluster you. Second, you've made my father's night and that makes me grateful beyond words. Third, I'd like the same kind of cone my dad has because you did a great sales job."

She angled him a saucy "I do what I can" kind of smile.

"And fourth, does Luke Campbell come around to bring you animal gifts on a regular basis?"

Piper's hand paused.

So did her heart.

And when it started again, she knew exactly what he was asking, and why all she wanted to do was flirt right back with him.

But her emotional scars stopped her.

Intellectually she knew her former fiancé's misdeeds had nothing to do with the broad-shouldered trooper at her ice cream window, but family embarrassment had dogged Piper for over a decade. She couldn't—wouldn't—put herself in the hot seat again. When she put cops in the "no dating" category, she'd meant it. But Zach didn't know that, and she could simply let his assumption about Luke ride. Easier on both of them.

And so she smiled softly and said, "Luke's a great guy, isn't he?"

Zach's gaze scanned her face. His eyes took in her easy expression, her gentle smile, and she let him read what she wanted him to see. Let him think she was off-limits. Because, despite the fact that Luke was just a good friend who lived on the opposite side of Kirkwood Lake, she was okay having Zach consider her off the market because she utterly refused to be fooled by a cop ever again. No matter how nicely he smiled.

CHAPTER THREE

"THERE IS A BICENTENNIAL COMMITTEE meeting tonight." Lucia tapped the calendar page with one blunt finger the following morning. Her voice said attending the meeting didn't make her short list, but they both knew one of them needed to be there to represent their farm.

"We can have Noreen stay late and help at the ice cream window." Piper tugged on socks, hating the heat but knowing her boots would chafe if she didn't layer up. "Can you check with her, see if that's okay? I'll go to the meeting," she continued. Lucia's quick smile rewarded her decision. "It's at seven, so just make sure I don't forget. And remind me in time to grab a quick shower, okay?"

"I'll text you. And Piper…" Lucia compressed her lips, a sure sign of trouble.

"What? What's happened?"

Lucia dipped her chin toward the west-facing window. "The Hogans are putting their farm on the market."

No.

Lucia breathed deep, watching her, because she understood the implications. Kirkwood Lake was becoming more populated. The beautiful lake, nestled between the rise of Enchanted Mountains and the lake plains of Lake Erie, had been overlooked for years during a depressed economy, but Piper had been approached by developers twice this past spring, both offering big bucks to turn McKinney Farm into an upscale subdivision with lake rights on the upper northwest shore.

Piper and Lucia had declined both offers, but Vince and Linda's farm sat above hers. The lake and quaint town sat below. As the Hogans aged, Piper's father had leased nearly eighty acres from them, acreage Piper used for corn. If the Hogans sold their farm, where would she find acreage for next year and the years to come, especially if increasing land values tempted more farmers out of the game?

"We'll figure this out." Lucia made the promise as if they had choices.

They didn't.

Piper crossed to the milking barn quickly. She'd oversee the morning chores with Berto, hope that Chas showed up to the dairy room on time, and try to accept the things she could not change, like the imminent For Sale sign in front of the neighboring farm.

Trouble was, she'd never grasped that life lesson well.

"Need a hand this morning?"

The disembodied voice startled Piper. She bit back a girly screech, then recognized Zach's father moving her way. "Mr. Harrison?"

"Call me Marty."

She raised one shoulder in acknowledgement, but the adrenaline rush of having him here in the shadowed dawn kept her heart pumping. "It's early for ice cream, isn't it?"

His smile reassured her. Dimmed hints of Zach's good looks and humor came through the softened expression. "Is it ever too early for ice cream?"

Piper shook her head, trying to feel the situation out and coming up short. "No. Not in my world, anyway."

Marty motioned to his right. "Zach's got a massive backyard project scheduled, so he's gone to the Home

Depot. I'm an early riser, I hate television and I worked on a farm for years. I'd like to help if you've got stuff to keep me busy."

Did she have stuff?

And then some.

But a cash shortfall made her keep the staff minimal to the point of negligible. "There's always work here. Compensation for that work is another matter," she told him as she moved into the barn. Berto lifted a hand in greeting as he tended the initial group of Holsteins, then he stood straighter, shoulders back, as he spotted the strange man at Piper's side. He moved their way, protective but open, qualities Piper loved about her middle-aged step-uncle.

"I don't need money," Zach's father told her.

Piper might be young, but she'd never met anyone who didn't need money. And Marty's clothes—which were somewhat loose and dated—said if he had money, he didn't spend it on his appearance. Which made his assertion more doubtful.

"Free help?" Berto defused the moment with a smile and waved Marty his way. "And I heard you say you have worked on a farm, no?"

"Yes."

Berto's expression said Marty had come to the right place. "He can work with me here," he told Piper.

Piper read what Berto wasn't saying, that he'd keep an eye on Marty and make sure things were on the level. Having a strange guy, a new neighbor, show up out of the blue wasn't the norm in Kirkwood.

It's not the norm anywhere, *her brain scolded.*

Mixed feelings made Piper hesitate. She didn't know this man.

You've met his son, the cop. How bad can he be?

"I'll take this side." Moving with more grace than Piper had observed the night before, Marty took a spot on the milking row opposite Berto. Without a glance in either direction, he began prepping the cows with a dexterity Piper almost envied.

Berto met her gaze. "We've got this."

Dismissed.

Which meant she could move the unfreshened heifers onto new pasture earlier than planned. She climbed into the pickup truck, headed west, turned the young cows out in record time, and was back to the house ninety minutes earlier than usual.

"You are back." Lucia frowned her way as she ladled pancake batter onto a hot griddle. Plump blueberries sizzled and burst in the heat, filling the air with sweet, summer fragrance. "The milking is done or the vacuum machine is broken?"

"Neither. Zach's dad came over to help. He and Berto are doing the milking."

"The policeman's father is working here?"

Piper made a face. "Weird, huh?"

Lucia set her gaze hard. "I have little trust for those who butt in to another's business."

"And yet you help so many, Lucia." Piper shrugged, grabbed coffee and buttered a steaming pancake. Then she took a sifter of powdered sugar, generously applied it to the pancake, rolled the whole thing into a cylinder and raised it to her mouth to bite. "You're always first in line to help with church functions or folks down on their luck."

"We are not down on anything that hard work and a heart for God won't fix." Lucia flipped the sizzling cakes with more zest and authority than could ever be needed. "We are independent. Industrious. Hardwork—"

"Whoa." Piper paused the pancake roll without a bite, and the scent of it, sugary-fruitiness waiting to be consumed, made her wish she could ignore Lucia's angst.

She couldn't. "Luce, he's not exactly breaching our

defenses. He's running milk lines to udders. And Berto's got things under control. Right?"

Lucia's frown said it wasn't right, but then her expression became subdued.

Piper turned.

Zach stood in the doorway much as he had two nights before, only this time thick concern worried his brow. "Have you guys seen my father? I had to run some errands at first light. He's not home and he's not the take-a-walk type. I wondered if he might have headed over here?"

"He did. We have him sequestered in the milking parlor, where he seems right at home, and you're just in time for food." Piper eyed the cooling rolled pancake in her hand and decided it was thoroughly gauche to eat a pancake like that in front of a great-looking guy, even if she had declared him off-limits. Swallowing a sigh, she started to put the pancake down as Zach stepped through the door.

"You roll your pancakes, too?"

"Too?"

He nodded, dipped a smile toward Lucia and slanted a questing gaze toward the plate. "May I?"

"Of course."

He repeated Piper's butter and sugar maneuvers, then rolled the cake tightly and took a bite. "Ah, Lucia. *Es muy delicioso.*"

Zach rolled his pancakes. Just as she did. That had to mean something, right?

Sure, her internal command center noted. *It means he's hungry. Leave it alone.* "Your father knows dairy cattle. Milking procedures. Why is that?"

Zach met her look directly. "I told you. I was a farm boy. Worked with my father for years."

"And this farm was...?"

"Central New York. About two hours east."

"And now—"

"Sold. Nearly two years ago."

She'd have to be blind or foolish to miss the note of regret in the lawman's eye, a resignation in his tone. Knowing the intricacy of maintaining a profitable farm, she had no trouble understanding how difficult that must have been for Marty. "I'm sorry. These are hard times."

Zach's gaze agreed, but he pasted a smile on his face as footsteps approached the back door. Piper took his cue and dropped the conversation. "Hey. You guys made record time. Marty, you're showing me up."

Berto kicked his boots off, came in and headed for the kitchen sink. He indicated Marty as if they were long-lost best friends. "Me, too. I had to move quickly to pretend to keep up."

His words put a smile on Marty's face, a genuine look of pleasure.

"Amazing pancakes." Zach made the pronouncement as he helped himself to another one. He paused, eyeing Piper's hand and the uneaten cake. "You haven't eaten yours."

"I will."

"It's cold." He swiped hers with an athlete's dexterity and handed her the hot, buttered cake roll he'd just made. "Eat this one while it's hot, because I don't make sacrifices casually."

She took a bite of the rolled-up pastry and agreed with him on one thing: the tubed cakes were fine cold, but they were melt-in-your-mouth delicious while warm.

But she didn't buy that he didn't make sacrifices casually. His job, his presence, the slightly careful attention he paid his father?

She was willing to bet Zach Harrison made casual sacrifices every single day but was too darned nice to know it.

Piper moved further into the town hall conference room that evening, but kept toward the rear purposely. Getting out quick at meeting's end meant getting home early, always a plus.

"I didn't expect to see you here," a new but familiar voice offered softly, far too close to her right ear to ignore. "We could have come down together."

Goose bumps prickled Piper's arms, and she didn't have to turn to know who was standing behind her at the crowded bicentennial planning meeting. After meeting him three days ago, Zach's voice had already found its way past her defenses. Not good. Not good at all.

"I walked down." She didn't turn so he moved closer, off to her right, his arm snug against hers in the crowded conditions. A good fire marshal would demand that thirty people, minimum, should leave because the room was grossly over-limit, but the fire marshal was on the board and knew how to pick his battles in their small town. "My great-great-grandparents were some of the original settlers."

"Generational farm."

"Yes." She turned to face him more fully, and recognized the bad move in record time. Away from him, it was easy to dismiss his breadth and solidity. That strong, stalwart commanding presence. In the abstract, she could write off his warmth, the humor in those bright blue eyes, the air of protection he carried intrinsically.

Up close now?

Not a chance.

He smiled down at her, and something in the ease of that grin called to her, but she'd been there, done that and wasn't about to repeat the mistake, especially in front of over one hundred townies as the meeting was called to order.

Twenty minutes in, Piper was glad she'd left Lucia home with the girls. Lucia's patience thinned with protocol, and by the time they'd waded through last month's minutes and changes, and voted on those changes, she was ready to head for the hills herself.

"Why don't they send the minutes out as an email, ask for adjustments, make those adjustments, then start the meeting with acceptance of the amended minutes?" Zach whispered the question into her right ear, having no idea what the tickle of breath did to her pulse.

"I dare you to make that suggestion."

He swept the aging crowd a look, then shrugged acceptance. "Gotcha."

"Uh-oh."

"What?" He leaned closer again. Piper pointed front and center where an aging woman with a really bad dye job stood, jabbing a finger toward the bicentennial board appointees.

"Violet Yardley, our resident revivalist. She's rich, owns land that straddles both counties and wants things her way."

"South shore, not far from Clearwater, adjacent to the vacant campgrounds."

"That's one of her properties. Yes. I take it you've patrolled down there?"

"Troopers, sheriffs and the occasional Clearwater cop have been called on-site, even though it's off the Clearwater jurisdiction. Empty cottages and spaced-out kids from the city make a bad combo. She wants to run the show here, huh?"

Piper slanted him a quick look of approval. "She can't, but she'll make a solid attempt."

He placed a strong but light hand on her shoulder, a touch that meant more when accompanied by his words. "Can't blame folks for trying, can you?"

"Blame, no." She met the twinkle in his gaze with a solid look of determination. "Refuse? Yes."

He heard the words. Read the look. And he wasn't foolish. He'd seen the careful way she'd handled his question about Luke Campbell the previous night, but for whatever reason, God seemed determined to put this woman in his path. Was it random chance that he bought the house abutting her farm? Or God's will?

He'd have declared "chance" three days ago. Now? He wasn't so sure. He'd seen his father smile. Rescued a miniature goat. Had his heart won by two little girls bent on mischief.

Whatever the reason, he liked Piper McKinney's company, but she'd shied away from him. Hint taken. He'd just had nearly two thousand dollars' worth of pressure-treated lumber delivered to his backyard. For the next two weeks, manual labor, power tools and the scent of sawdust would mark his time. With his father's help, maybe they could complete the project in the next thirteen days, leaving his hunting season vacation intact. And maybe it would get Marty's mind off his change of circumstance.

"Do we have representatives from law enforcement here this evening?" The board chairman scanned the crowd as he asked the question.

"Here." Zach raised a hand, drawing attention from the surrounding room. And with that attention, he noted that more than one person saw him standing closer than was necessary to Piper McKinney. "Trooper Zach Harrison, New York State Police."

"And here." From the other side of the room Luke Campbell's older brother also raised a hand. He made a visual but silent connection with Zach, then turned toward the board. "Deputy Sheriff Seth Campbell. Once the committee firms its plans, Trooper Harrison and I will present our strategy on public safety that will take us through the bicentennial year."

"You're working the bicentennial?" Piper looked up at him, and he had to pretend it didn't affect him. "You hadn't mentioned that before."

"I do believe our conversations have centered on raucous birds, tiny goats, cherry ice cream and cows. I don't think my job has once entered into the mix. Why is that, Piper?"

She flashed a smile. "I talk faster than you."

"There's that." He drawled the words purposely, giving her time. Hoping she'd open up, just a little. But why was he hopeful? What was there about her that drew him?

"And my farm life is fascinating and all-encompassing, and spares me time for little else."

"I will shrug off the first, chart the second as personal choice, and the third as a cool put-off."

"Whereas I'd call it life and be done with it. We are what we are, we do what we do and life moves on accordingly."

The annoyance in her tone gave Zach more to chew on.

The meeting adjourned after several progress reports. As folks moved to the exits, an older man came to a stop in front of Piper. Sadness and resignation filled his eyes. "I expect you've heard."

She nodded, reached out and hugged him. "Vince, you do what you have to do. You need to take care of you and Linda."

"I shoulda offered it to you first before signin' with that realty place, though." He twisted his hands, penitent. "I promised your daddy I'd do that."

Piper shrugged off his apology with a gentle grace Zach envied. "I don't have the money to buy your land, Vince. You knew that. You saved me an awkward moment."

The man's face relaxed a little. "Mother said much the

same thing, but it's good to hear it straight from you. Where will you plant your corn now?"

"We'll find a place," Piper assured him. "We always do, don't we?"

"Yes." The man smiled, eager to agree, guilt eased. "Farmers always find a way." He nodded up to Zach and moved off.

Zach stepped in front of Piper, blocking her way to the door of the emptying room, forcing her to face him. "That was a nice thing you did."

She shrugged.

Her attempt to slough off the compliment deepened his smile. "Where *will* you plant your corn?"

She bit her lip and frowned. "I have no idea. He's the second farmer on the west side to fold this year. The town resurgence is wonderful, but it inflates land values like crazy."

Zach understood that. Their family farm had sold for an outrageous sum of money, cash they thought they'd need to take care of Marty. Only now he was healthy and had money in the bank, and no farm.

By default and proximity, Zach had been the elected decision-maker, which made the situation with his father mostly his fault. The fact that he hadn't loved the farm was no big secret. Did his father think he'd made that decision casually?

"How big is their place?" He looked toward the exit, where Vince was met by a pretty blonde grandmotherly type who hooked her arm with his.

"Ninety acres. Nearly ten of them are woodlands and hedgerow, but the other eighty we've kept prime for nearly a dozen years. Great slope, good drainage, not too rocky. Oops, sorry." She made a face, cute and regretful. "More farm talk."

"I'm getting used to it. Again."

His wry note made her smile and he liked that, watching her face light up and the furrow in her brow smooth out.

It softened her dogged determination, too, the firm set of her chin and shoulders as she tackled tasks a lot of men would hire out. The softer side held great appeal. The tougher, no-nonsense face she showed more often?

That reminded him too much of his father, tied to the land, the cows, twenty-four/seven. He'd lived that once and hated it. He never wanted to live it again.

"Harrison?"

Zach turned as Seth Campbell approached them. "Seth. How are you?"

"I'd be better if you answered your emails," the deputy replied, but he mellowed the words with a smile.

"Took an unexpected leave," Zach told him. "Text me, instead. Or just call my cell. There's not much we can do until they firm up the bicentennial schedule, though, right?"

"True. I was just checking in to see if you'd be here tonight. Piper. How's everything going? All this heat and no rain making you crazy yet?"

She whacked his arm in a manner that suggested old friends. "No more so than people asking me if the heat and lack of moisture is making me crazy."

He laughed. "I ran into Chas yesterday."

"And got an earful, no doubt."

"And then some. I told him to branch out, look for other work if he hates the farm so much. That's what you did, right?" Seth settled a frank look toward Zach.

A moment of silence stretched on before Piper turned her attention up. A new level of understanding deepened the green of her irises.

Zach fumbled the moment. "I knew I needed a different kind of work, yes." His reply sounded lame, even to him, because he knew she'd focused on one key phrase, "hates the farm". Being an honest man, he wasn't about to deny it.

"Farming's not for everyone." Piper stepped back, ready to distance herself. Surrounding herself with negative farm talk was in no one's best interest, especially hers. She was a numbers gal; she understood the fine line between success and failure. But life and faith had taught her to avoid negative energy and seek the bright side of things. An optimist?

Yes, with a realist's work ethic, and she wasn't about to let anyone's unenthusiastic take on her chosen profession bring her down. Not when her balance was already precarious. "Gentlemen." She started up the road that led toward the farm with a quick wave of dismissal. "I've got to get back home. Nice seeing you."

"You too, Piper."

Seth's voice followed her.

Zach's stayed silent. Just as well, because there was little to say. She'd noted his aversion to farming right off. He'd hated the roosters, the noise, the confusion surrounding her. She sensed that instantly. So why did she let a pair of sweet blue eyes confound her? What was wrong with her? Why couldn't she move on accordingly?

Lesson learned. From this point forward she'd consider herself forewarned. Unapproachable. Off-limits and immune to Zach's strength and sincerity.

The "come hither" blue eyes?

She sighed, pushing herself to walk faster. The magnetic pull of those eyes put her right back in the hot seat every time. What was she going to do about that?

CHAPTER FOUR

"HEY."

A hand touched Piper's arm less than a hundred yards later.

She screeched, a feminine "just saw a mouse" squeak.

"I called your name. You didn't turn," Zach smiled at her, and his look said her surprise was her own fault.

"Call louder next time." She scowled, pulled her arm back and looked behind him. "You forgot your car."

"I walked, too. You didn't give me time to say that during the meeting."

"Oh."

"And I thought since we're walking in the same direction, we could walk together."

Try as she might, she could not argue with that.

"And you were quietly storming off because I didn't like being raised on a farm, and I thought we might want to talk about that."

"Except…" She held up a hand, palm out. "Your choices have no effect on either one of us. We're neighbors and we'll live compatibly side by side, but that's it."

"You're sure?" He took her raised hand in both of his in a touch so gentle, so pure, that her heart wanted to melt on the spot. His gaze lingered on the calluses, the short nails, the dry, rough skin. He didn't bring her hand to his mouth for a kiss, but his expression *was* a kiss, a look of warmth and tenderness, longing to help.

Then he made a slight grimace, released her hand, and started walking next to her.

"Zach, I don't flirt well."

He laughed. "Yes, you do."

"Okay, maybe I do," she amended honestly. "But I shouldn't. Won't."

"Me, either. Maybe sometime we should sit down and list our reasons, Piper, because even though I've only known you a few days, and I live just around the corner, when I'm not with you, I'm thinking about you."

"Well, stop."

He laughed again. "I've tried. It doesn't appear to be working."

"Try harder."

"Part of me doesn't want to."

They'd reached the driveway leading up to the farmhouse. She heard what he was saying, but she'd learned to harden her heart to sweet-talking overtures a few years ago. And only a fool would leave herself wide open for heartbreak from another cop and a neighbor besides.

A farm-hating neighbor, at that.

The lowing of contented cattle drifted their way. The roosters were tucked away for the night. The hens, too, the dimmer light pushing them to their roosts. A soft breeze and cooler temperatures made the evening less oppressive. Piper turned her face into the breeze, letting it cool the heat of walking nearly three-quarters of a mile uphill. "I love this place."

Zach watched her, silent.

"And I've had to fight for ten years to keep it going. I took college courses nearby so I could live at home and work the farm. I watched my parents' marriage fall apart because she hated this life. Did you know there's a website now, a singles site, for farmers? Because the divorce rate among farmers is so high? And it's nearly impossible for a guy to find a woman who wants to be tied to the rigors of farm life. The daily sacrifices it entails. For a woman?" She worked her jaw, then shrugged. "I've learned the hard way to put my future in God's hands. Most days." She sent him a smile of admission. "And in all honesty, I'm usually too busy to care."

She took a broad step back, hands raised, a move that negated his step forward. "I have more than a job here. I have a legacy. And I get that most people don't understand it, but I've spent a lot of time seeking faith and guidance on this stuff. I take nothing lightly when it comes to this farm. This family." She looked left when the laughter of children floated across the dancing grass in need of mowing. "Lucia. Berto. My brothers. The twins. Noreen and Marly in the ice cream shop. Every decision I make affects them, and I can't afford to make more mistakes." She backpedaled up the drive and sent him a small smile and a quick wave. "I think your dad's coming over to work tomorrow. If that's okay."

"My father can do whatever he wants." Zach's expression said her words surprised him. "He doesn't need my permission for anything."

"Does he know that?"

Aggravation hit him because she was right, and that frustrated him.

He'd been treating his father with kid gloves because of Marty's health issues, but his father was better now. And Zach had to learn to back off. Be the kid.

And that was hard for a grown man who wore a badge and carried a gun.

He wanted to watch Piper walk to the house.

He didn't.

He strode up and around the corner, past the pond, not

stopping for a cone, or a talk with the kids, or to pet the little goat.

Right now, he wanted to create distance between him and most everything on the planet.

A slight sound caught his attention.

He turned, the late-day shadows playing tricks with his eyes.

The noise came again, imploring. Needy.

Puppies.

His mother had bred golden retrievers for years. He'd know that sound anywhere.

His heart softened, then hardened as he approached a bag tossed alongside the pond. Hard stillness marked one side of the bag, but the movement within the tied sack gave him hope. He bent low, withdrew the sack from the water's edge and untied it carefully.

Four tiny puppies mewled up at him, eyes shut tight, days old. Tossed aside like yesterday's garbage.

Someone had weighted the bag with a rock and tossed it into the pond area, but missed the water by inches. Then they'd driven off, leaving the pups to bake in the summer sun.

"What've you got there?"

Marty approached him with an ice cream cone in hand, his brows up-thrust.

"Puppies."

"No." Marty's face went hard and soft, just like Zach's had done. "They dumped them?"

"Tried for the pond. Missed."

"Good thing you came 'round this way," Marty told him. "I wondered why you didn't come over for ice cream, but if you had, these little guys would be goners."

A spark of wisdom nudged Zach. "What can we do with them, Dad?"

"Save 'em, of course." Marty handed off the cone to Zach and cradled the bag in his arms as if he carried something rare and precious. "Your mother loved puppies."

"She did." The regret in his father's voice stirred up something else inside Zach. "Even though they were a bother."

"I shouldn't have said that," his father confessed as he carried the puppies toward their house. "The dogs were her project. And it was her farm, too. I should have praised that more, because those pups brought in a pretty penny at times when we needed it."

Marty's words said Zach wasn't the only Harrison who harbored regrets. "Mom was pretty independent. I don't think she was looking for praise."

"I should have given it, in any case," Marty told him. "I knew it then, I know it now. Run over to the farm and see if Piper's got any baby animal supplement. If not, bring me some fresh milk and I'll condense it to make formula for these guys. And see if she's got eyedroppers, too."

Run to the farm?

See Piper?

The woman who just brushed him off?

The sight of Marty hunting up a small box, lining it with an old towel, then tucking it into a darkened corner was enough to push Zach across the field. He'd find Piper, make his father's request and then head home, ready to take her advice. He'd be foolish to waste time searching for common ground. From now on his common ground with Piper McKinney was property lines, drawn by surveyors required for his mortgage.

Neighbors.

That was that. A deck to build was more than enough to fill his vacation time. Backbreaking work under a blazing summer sun would put thoughts of Piper where they belonged: out of sight, out of mind.

"Puppies? Dumped? Are you kidding me, Zach? Who would do that?"

Piper's maternal expression put Zach right back in the zone he'd decried not minutes before, which meant he really needed to work harder to put her out of his thoughts. "Dad was wondering if you had anything over here to help raise them. If we can save them, that is."

"I don't, but Luke will." She pulled out her phone, hit a number on her speed dial, and was connected to Luke Campbell in seconds.

But it was plenty long enough for Zach to read the writing on the wall.

Campbell liked animals.

He had a cute kid.

He'd been widowed for over two years.

He was a nice guy.

And he had baby puppy formula supplement. That took a first-place blue ribbon right there.

Zach stopped the list of attributes before it grew any longer. If Campbell and Piper were a done deal, he needed to face reality.

Luke and his little boy pulled into Piper's yard fifteen minutes later. He retrieved a bag of supplies while his son, Aiden, climbed out of the booster seat in back.

Piper approached him, apologetic. "I hope you didn't have to get Aiden out of bed. One of us—" she nodded in Zach's direction "—could have come over and picked it up."

Luke noogied his son's head. "Bedtime's late this time of year, and I promised him ice cream. That made hopping into the car a quick deal."

Piper smiled down at the little boy. "I would do most anything for ice cream, too, kid. Do you want to go play with the girls?"

Aiden shook his head, shy. He leaned into his father's leg as if seeking support.

"He can hang with us." Luke sent a smile of approval to the boy. "Where are the puppies?"

"His place." Piper motioned to Zach as she moved toward the cut-through between the barns. "Zach, do you know Luke?"

"We met at the breast cancer run last October, and on the Whitehorse Café case. And I'm working the bicentennial with your brother Seth." Zach reached out a hand, shook Luke's and tried to make his greeting something other than tepid.

He failed. Miserably.

But Luke's smile said he was oblivious to Zach's true feelings. "I remember. You busted loose and won the race, and gave the sheriff's department necessary info to nail the guy who trashed the café. You live over here?"

"Moved in a few weeks ago. I got to meet an old friend of yours, I hear." Zach squatted to Aiden's level as he indicated the far barn with a quick look to the right. "Beansy the goat."

The little boy's eyes shone. His quick nod made Zach smile. But he stayed quiet, his grip tight on his father's hand.

They moved into Zach's house and Piper winced slightly. "It *is* hot in here."

"Hah." Zach shot her an "I told you so" look that she shrugged off.

"It's cooler down here," Marty called. He'd tucked the pups into the second-lowest level of the house.

"Would the basement be better, Dad?" Zach wondered. "It's even cooler there."

"Pups this age like eighty degrees," Marty told them. "My wife bred dogs for years. She was finicky about keeping the temps hiked until they were two weeks old because they lose heat quickly."

"No fur."

"Right. What've we got here?" Marty shifted his gaze from Piper to Luke.

"Eyedroppers, puppy supplement, disposable gloves, nail trimmers and baby wipes for their bottoms. And a recipe for making your own supplement in a few days. This is good for starters, but pricey."

"Well, let's get started." Marty handed them each an eyedropper, popped the top on a can of formula and bent low. "I'll start with this little fella."

He picked up a tiny male pup with tender hands, then gained Luke's approval by dropping a bead of milk on the pup's upper lip, allowing the pup to find the milk with his tongue. It took several drops before the pup hunted for the source of the milk, but once he did, the pup pursed his tiny mouth avidly, drawing drops of food from the plastic tube.

"Don't overfeed this first time," Luke counseled. "Give them a little, let their bodies adjust."

"Exactly right." Marty shot him a look of approval. "You know things about pups."

"Or I'm a sucker for baby animals." Luke smiled, stood and rolled his shoulders.

Aiden tugged his hand, drawing Luke's attention down. He smiled and rubbed the boy's head. "You want to see Beansy?"

The boy nodded.

"And get ice cream before Lucia closes things up?"

Aiden's grin said his father read him clearly. "You guys are all right here?"

Piper nodded as she crooned murmurs of love to the minute creature in her hand, the sound making Zach long to draw closer. But that would be stupid and shortsighted, so he stood along with Luke and moved toward the half-flight of stairs rising to the main level.

"Be sure to rub their tummies," Luke added as he and Aiden moved up the steps.

"Will do." Piper shot him a look of gratitude. "Thanks for running right over."

"Glad to help."

Zach followed Luke and Aiden out the door. The cooler air felt good against his face. "Thanks, Luke. You're welcome to wait for Piper here, you know."

"Wait for...?" Luke turned, his face questioning, and in that gaze Zach read exactly what he hoped to see. "I'll see her at the house. Or the next time we stop by."

An interested man would never brush off time with a woman like Piper. Zach understood that, and he shouldn't be the least bit happy that Luke's casual expression said there was nothing between him and the farmer next door. But he was happy. Very.

Luke eyed him, then smiled. "You thought I had something going with Piper."

"Just didn't want to get in anyone's way," Zach countered.

Luke laughed out loud. "Well, if you can get by Piper McKinney's cop-phobic attitude, more power to you. Her old fiancé did quite a number on her, and Piper doesn't have much use for cops these days."

Zach's arched brow invited Luke to continue, but Luke shook his head. "Not my story to tell, because Piper's a good friend and has been for years, but if you do an internet search on Hunter Reilich, you'll understand why she shies away from uniforms. Between her and Lucia, they don't have a lot of trust in the system right now."

Reilich? The dirty cop who aided and abetted a racketeering ring after his father bought his way into the Clearwater Police Department?

Zach had noted Lucia's reticence. But Piper's?

He hadn't seen that coming.

He remembered the story. Reilich was a seven-year veteran with lofty family connections and a lust for power. He got brought down after several police agencies received an anonymous tip about his shady dealings. Reilich and a handful of others were indicted and convicted for their actions. Their bust made it possible for the Buffalo police to partner with the FBI and the state troopers to dismantle a widespread drug ring in Western New York. The mountainous terrain made it pretty easy to hide things like meth labs. Gambling dens. Drug houses.

Disgust mingled with surprise inside him. Piper and a guy like Reilich?

He'd mull that over later. Right now he stooped low and held out a hand to Aiden. "Thanks for coming to see the puppies. Come over again, okay?"

The boy's tenuous smile as he gripped his daddy's leg said he'd like to visit the pups again. Zach moved back up a step as Luke started toward the ice cream barn. "Luke, thanks."

"Any time. I'll stop back in a day or two, see how they're doing. If that's all right?"

"It's fine."

"As long as I don't have designs on a certain farmer," Luke added, grinning.

"You're a quick study, Campbell." Zach gave him a half-wave, half-salute goodbye. "We'll see you soon."

Piper met him halfway to the stairs. "Luke's gone?"

"Headed to your place for ice cream. So no. Not really."

"The pups are sleeping for the moment." She smiled at Zach's father as he quietly climbed the stairs behind her. "Luke said to feed them about every two hours, right?"

"For the first week. We can take shifts." Marty met Zach's gaze over Piper's head.

"Or do it together in half the time," Zach supposed.

His words made his father smile. "Your mother would have seen it that way, too."

Janet Harrison liked people, she sought company, she loved baby creatures. In some ways Zach was like her. But his dogged determination to handle a job, get it done and do it right?

That was Marty, through and through. Only Zach had sense enough to know when to walk away. Come home. Chill out.

Piper reached out and hugged Marty. The embrace surprised the older man, but he returned the hug. "Marty, I'm so glad you found those little guys."

"I didn't. Zach did."

"Oh." She turned, taken aback. Her fumble made Zach grin.

"Do I get a hug now?"

"No."

Zach feigned an arrow to the heart. "I'm wounded."

She ignored his antics and moved to the door. "Marty, call me if you need me."

"You have enough to do," Marty told her. He used his no-nonsense voice, the one that said he'd be fine. No help needed. "I'll be over to help tomorrow. Between feedings, that is. And no sense telling me no, young lady. I like to keep busy."

"Thank you, Marty." She sent him a smile as she stepped through the door.

Zach followed her. Walked her down the steps. Then across the yard, hands thrust into his pockets. If he could whistle, he would, because knowing Luke Campbell didn't have feelings for the petite farmer at his side made him happy.

"What are you doing?" Piper's voice held a sigh of resignation that said she knew exactly what he was doing, but would call him on it anyway.

"Walking a pretty lady home."

"Umm…" She directed her gaze forward and waved a hand. "In case you haven't noticed, I am home."

"A gentleman always walks a lady to her door."

"Zach—"

He paused. Faced her.

She dug a toe into the ground and looked away.

With one gentle finger he drew her face back, toward him. "I like you. I like being nice to you. There's no law against that and I'm a cop, so I'm an expert on law and order. Let's leave it at that for now, okay?"

"But it doesn't get left at that," she whispered, and it hurt him to hear the raw note in her voice. "Things happen, and they happen more often around cops. I'm no fan of drama. All I want is a normal life, a greeting-card-commercial existence. And Zach?" She stepped away from his touch, from his gaze. "My life has been anything but, so you might want to think hard and fast yourself."

"You're warning me off."

Her sad, resolute smile became more grim. "I'm warning us both off."

"Piper."

"Gotta go." She turned and jogged the rest of the way to the house. The light slap of the wooden screen door said she was in. Safe.

But he'd read the expression on her face. Heard the note of wistful resignation in her tone. Whatever had gone on with this family did a number on her. And he hated to see her weighted down with work. He might not love farming, but he had the muscle and the know-how to help her. That would be the Christian thing to do. Speak your faith, live your faith, love one another. A fairly simple concept.

His internal warning system clicked into high gear. Leave it alone. You have plenty to do and no love of farming.

She's got a farm to run and no big appreciation for cops. The writing's on the wall. All you have to do is read it.

The caution hit home. Zach had bought a house in a country setting because he liked room to roam and land to hunt come autumn. He started the summer with a plan. There was work to be done. That deck wasn't going to build itself.

He and Marty had clashed on the family farm more than once. Better to let his father help Piper while he worked at home. Ripping out over two hundred feet of bad wood should keep his mind from wandering. Adding four tiny puppies to the mix should ensure it.

CHAPTER FIVE

"TRACTOR DOWN. MARTY HELPING. CAN u milk alone?"

Piper glared at the text as she rolled to a stop alongside the near barn later that week.

Fields of what should be lush thigh-high corn looked stressed. The corn's struggle reflected Piper's emotions. She parked the truck by the far barn, hopped out and headed for the milking shed.

"Piper."

Colin's voice caught her attention. He moved her way purposefully, and Piper read his body language. He wasn't looking for a fight, as Chas often did, but he wanted to press home a point. The set of his shoulders and chin made that clear, even from a distance. "What's up?"

"We've had another offer on the farm."

His words sent a roll of anger snowballing through her. "We've?"

He looked to the right, indicating the dairy store. "A developer approached me and Chas."

Because you're the weak link, and the developer specializes in ferreting information about each family.

Unfortunately, the developer's strategy had worked on other farm families already. "You explained that the farm isn't for sale, right?"

"We asked them to name a price."

Piper understood the inflated cost of housing and land in their area. The lakeside setting offered a host of possibilities. Docks, boat slips, swimming areas, the list went on and on. But when Colin named the price they'd offered, she had to take a moment to regroup.

"That's crazy talk."

"They said we can keep the house and the barns," her brother countered. "Plus the five acres surrounding it. So you and Lucia could buy us out and still live there pretty cheap."

Buy them out of her home?

Buy them out of the place she'd worked day and night to save while they complained about every little thing, two college-educated guys who rarely looked for work off the farm and did precious little to help on the farm?

The anger grew.

"You've got it all figured out." She faced him, forcing him to meet her gaze. "You and Chas take your cut of the family legacy while Lucia and I are left with a house and barns but no farm. What exactly are we supposed to do with that, Colin?"

"I—"

"I'll tell you what you can do with your developer's offer." She stepped closer, undeterred by the size difference and her brother's take-charge attitude. "Tell them McKinney Farm isn't for sale. Not now. Not ever. And then go look for a job, like normal people do."

"Kiera's pregnant."

He didn't offer the news like a proud, young father. He dropped the words like a man doomed, as if the worst-case scenario had just fallen on him.

"Doesn't that make you happy?" Piper didn't try to hide the disbelief in her tone. A baby should be cause to sing praise. Not a punishment.

"She'll have to take time off to have the baby." Colin's expression said the very idea of Kiera using time to give birth rocked the world as he knew it, and that only aggravated Piper more. "And it's not all covered by insurance."

Piper took a deep, slow breath, wondering how she and her brothers could possibly be related. Then she remembered how her mother shrugged off her responsibilities in a callous disregard for her family.

Obviously Piper took after her father, a land-lover, a person of industry. Ambitious and strong. Faithful to a fault.

The boys were more like their mother. Cool. Dismissive. Looking for the easy way out. Well, there was no easy way out of this. She wasn't about to step back and let them have their way. She and Lucia had stood strong so far. They'd do it again. Without Rainey the vote was tied, 2-2. Unless the farm went bankrupt and they were forced to sell, Piper and Lucia would hang tight.

"Vince and Linda will sell their place." Colin folded his arms, his tone tough. "You'll lose nearly eighty productive acres of rental land. You can't run a dairy operation with no feed. No room for cash crops. No grain in the silos. So maybe you better think about this, Piper. You talk about me getting a job." He sent her work clothes a look of disgust. "Maybe you should get off the farm, see the world from someplace other than the seat of a tractor and get a life. At least I don't use the farm as a place to hide."

He strode away, not waiting for a response, and that was all right, because Piper couldn't trust herself to speak just then.

She moved into the barn, ready to smack the first thing that got in her way. Unfortunately for Zach, it was him.

"Hey." He dodged the backswing of the side door into the milking parlor and threw his hands up in the air. "Whoever you're mad at, remember: I didn't do it."

His presence surprised her. How did he know she'd be milking the cows alone?

He tapped his pocket. "Dad texted me. Said they were in a jam up the road."

Quick tears made her eyes smart. Extra help had become nonexistent once she'd lost her father, so this overture loosened a hard knot in her heart. "Give me five minutes."

"Or what?" He watched her, and the look on his face was caring. Maybe even tender.

It said he'd do whatever she asked, and that made the tears of anger she was fighting almost overflow. But not quite. "Or I'll lash out irrationally and you'll be the target for no other reason than geographical logistics."

His quick smile said he got it. "Being in the wrong place at the wrong time?"

"Yes." She scrubbed up, pulled on a pair of disposable gloves and moved forward. "Five minutes gives me time to think and pray. That way, no one gets hurt."

"I'm okay with that." He put one hand to her arm as she stepped toward the milking area, a hand that felt warm and strong and good. "But say the word, and I'll deck whoever made you mad."

His pledge of protection dissolved some of her angst. She sent him a quick smile of thanks and moved forward.

Colin had gone for the jugular, because he knew the score. Without land to grow crops, the farm would fail. The boys would win. And her family heritage would be lost forever. And there wasn't a thing she could do about it.

Zach read Piper's face as she banged through the side door. There was anger. Aggravation.

A part of him longed to soothe the angst away. Another part recognized the frustration of farming in her expression. He'd seen the same emotions on his father's face, countless times. For hardworking people, that lack of control of things such as weather and prices could spell the difference between success and failure.

Zach liked stability. Set hours. Money in the bank. A sure paycheck, deposited regularly. And he'd been bent over the old deck for nearly two days, sawing, prying, digging out stubborn nails and stripped screws. Every muscle in his body ached, but he'd come straight over when Marty texted him, because milking this many cows was a two-man job.

He moved quietly as they worked, the low sounds of a satisfied herd calming the moment. He patted a dark red flank as he released his first group of twelve out to the feed deck. "Recessive genes. Did you use a Canadian bull for that?"

"Mutant-R, actually." Piper didn't turn his way, but she sounded more at ease. Exactly what he was hoping for. "But once we threw a bull with the mutation, I kept him and worked on developing a line of red-and-whites. And you're talking."

He smiled as the first group of cows walked past him, their accustomed routine making the job of handling huge animals pretty simple. "I was hoping enough time had passed."

She made a face, assessing, then shrugged. "I suppose it has. I can always count on the girls—" she looked at the retreating cows "—to calm me down. They're so docile. Placid. Utterly content."

"*Utterly* content?" He made a face that made her laugh. "Please tell me you didn't just say that."

"Only another farm kid would recognize it," she quipped back. She moved to let the next group into the parlor as Zach closed the far gate. The cows filed in, each one moving to its place.

"I've always wondered." Zach indicated the row of bovines with a quizzical look. "Does this make them smart or stupid? To come in, day after day, knowing their place, going to it, walking step by step through life without looking right or left most of the time?"

"They're content." She moved down the row, making sure each udder was washed before drying the tender skin and attaching the vacuum milking suction cups. "Being satisfied with where you are isn't a bad thing." She gazed at him from her spot at the end of the milking channel. "Not everyone wants to be higher, faster, stronger. Richer."

"So it's a money thing that broadsided you."

"I knew you were groping for answers." She finished her row and stepped across the channel to work on his. "My brothers were offered a crazy amount for this farm. And the oldest couldn't wait to greet me with the news, let me know that Lucia and I are persona non grata."

Zach had sold their family farm for a seven-figure amount two years ago, so he understood the concept of rising land values. Piper's farm, with hundreds of feet of lake frontage below the curving, lakeshore road that ran through her property?

Astronomical.

As a non-farmer, he empathized with Piper's brother. However, if Zach's brother or sister had wanted to run the farm, he'd have done whatever he could to help them achieve that goal. Not stand in the way of their progress. "He hates farming."

"More like work-phobic."

Zach shot her a look of understanding. He'd known many a lazy soul in his time on the planet, and in his line of work it wasn't a big deal. Lazy cops got weeded out or passed over for promotions and eventually left the force.

But there was no place for laziness on a farm. Farms often had side businesses to balance the bad times. Piper's dairy store was a perfect example of that. "But one of them works in the dairy store, right? Processing the milk?"

"Only because they want to keep an eye on me. Make sure I don't ruin their inheritance with my ineptitude."

A thrum of anger stretched Zach's shoulders wider. Tighter. "They don't trust you?"

"They don't trust anyone. Partially with good reason." She shrugged, but said no more. "Mostly because they think if they can get their hands on their portion of this farm in cold, hard cash—"

Zach watched as she tried to explain their selfishness away, and realized it took a rare person to step back and look at the big picture when faced with this much negativity.

"...their lives can begin anew."

"With no regard to your life. Or the family farm."

"In their estimation, I have no life." She worked down her row of cows as she talked, her ponytail bobbing as she moved from cow to cow. "But they're wrong. I wouldn't trade my life for anything in the world. I love what I do."

"It shows."

She flashed him a smile, then made a face at him. "Your cows are really wishing they could get to food. My side is quietly making fun of yours."

He couldn't deny that she moved through the milking parlor like the expert she was. His father had been the same way. "Would expanding your herd help the financial side of things?"

She considered his question as her group filed out. "Yes, if I had more help. No, if it means I sleep less. Right now, sleep and family life are nonexistent. And that's the downside of my current situation."

"No time with the twins."

"Exactly." She waited to turn on the automatic floor washer until his group had left the area. "I feel guilty every time I see a notice for an activity I can't take the girls to. I don't want to deprive them of learning opportunities, but there's never enough time or money. They're starting school this fall. It will be the first time they've ever been separated, and I'm not sure who's more worried about that. Them or me."

"Kids are survivors."

"I know." Something in her tone told Zach she got that part. Maybe too well. "But sometimes they should just get to be kids, right?"

He moved to open the gate for the next group of cows just as Marty entered the milking parlor from the side door. He spotted Zach and stopped, surprised. "You were able to help."

"I was ready for a break from dry rot. And I'd just fed the pups."

"How are they doing?" Piper asked. "They're okay?"

"Thriving." Marty's expression showed pride. "I used to tease my wife about taking care of those baby dogs, how she'd pamper them. Right now I'm glad I paid attention."

"Me too." Piper's smile inspired Marty's in return, and for the first time since being released from the hospital, Marty seemed happy. More content. Having the pups on hand, and helping Piper on her farm, well…the two factors seemed to be helping Marty get back to his old self.

"I'm going to have a look at that tractor." He thrust his hands into his pockets. "Now don't tell me no, young lady, because I've been itching to get my hands on those old-style mechanics. That John Deere might have a few years under its belt, but it's a workhorse engine and I plan on making it purr like a kitten before I'm through. Then I'm taking a crack at the New Holland rig."

"Marty, you don't have to do that," she protested, but Zach wasn't blind to the glimmer of hope in her eye.

"Not have to. *Want* to. And then I'm going to have a look at your generators. If we get a storm and lose power, that's a lot of milk to dump. And make sure your partner over there—" he pointed Zach's way as he headed out

"—strips that milk properly. I spent a lot of years checking up on him."

A childish part of Zach wanted to offer a sharp comeback, but when his father shot him a teasing look, he realized the older Harrison was just being funny.

Why had he forgotten his father's sense of humor? When had he made the firm separation from father and farmer in his head?

"I think he does a great job." Piper aimed a smile Zach's way, a warm look that offered total appreciation for his presence. And the way her eyes met his?

That made milking nearly twelve dozen cows way more fun than it had ever been at home. That would give him something to think about as he started laying new lumber for his deck.

"There she is!"

"Ask her! Ask her!"

"We've been spotted," Zach told Piper as they exited the milking parlor later than afternoon. "But don't worry, I've got your back," he whispered in her ear as Dorrie and Sonya raced toward them. "It's two on two. I think we can take 'em."

The feel of his breath on her skin pulled her closer. But closer wasn't an option, so she stepped away and bent to the girls' level. "What's up?"

"The carnival!"

"Coming here!"

"This week!"

"And a parade!"

The twins' revelations proclaimed their excitement. Piper looked from one to the other, wondering how to tell them no. The parade was free, therefore affordable. The fireman's carnival with rides, games, food, all for a good cause? That was a no-go. If she counter-offered them the Friday night parade, maybe they wouldn't realize what they were missing.

"I've been waiting to go on that big wheel all my life," Dorrie exclaimed.

"And I want to pick ducks," Sonya added. "Like, maybe, five of them."

"And eat popcorn," Dorrie added.

"And drink pop." Sonya's eyes rounded at the idea. "With a bendy straw."

Sipping pop from a bendable straw was clearly big-league in five-year-old circles, but they'd have to settle for chocolate milk here on the farm. That wasn't such a bad thing, was it?

"When would you like to go?"

Zach's words pulled Piper's attention his way. He put a hand to her shoulder, a palm that felt rugged, warm, sweet and strong, then swept a look from the twins to her. "Saturday afternoon? Because Friday night after the parade will be really crowded."

"Um, I—"

"Sure you can." He nixed any rebuttal she might have offered by giving the near barn a quick glance. "Dad will gladly sub for whatever you'd like to accomplish on Saturday. You said you'd like the girls to be able to do more things, and I'm paying, so your excuses just ran dry."

"But—" He met her eyes with a take-charge look. His words hit home. Was she looking for reasons to be busy? Afraid to go out and face the world as her brother had intimated?

Dorrie and Sonya tugged her hands, breathless. Hopeful. Wide-eyed. "Yes. We'll do it. Saturday afternoon. But you don't have to pay," she scolded as she stood up. The twins danced around them, then raced for the house, shouting their news. "I can squeak money out of the grocery budget."

"My treat. End of discussion. You've fed us twice this past week. Consider it payback."

"Feeding you is the least we can do for all the free labor your father has given us. I"ll cover Saturday's costs." Piper tried to stand her ground, but couldn't. Zach had folded his arms and braced his feet slightly apart in a cop stance, strong and unbending. She hated that his take-charge attitude appealed to her, that his quiet, funny personality made him seem approachable. She'd seen enough of police to know that some cops wore a facade the way she wore barn boots.

He tweaked her nose, a tiny touch, sweet and almost cute, which made her want to deck him for making this attraction more difficult to ignore. "I pay. But if you're worried about leveling the playing field, you could wear that sundress I saw hanging on the line yesterday. The one with—"

"I know which one." She raised her gaze to his and stood, facing him, quiet and still. His next words surprised her.

"I'm not Reilich."

He knew.

Shame coursed through her, then anger.

What did Zach know of her? Of her family? Her father's death, her mother's departure, her engagement to Hunter? Rainey's imprisonment? The twins' birth and abandonment?

Here he was, a seemingly nice, normal guy who appeared to be a good cop. A man with a great father, whose work ethic matched her own. A guy from a salt-of-the-earth family with morals and ethics. The great biceps were simply icing on the cake.

She took a step back, hands up, palms out. "Clearly you are unaware of my first rule of business: no family talk. That includes incarcerated former fiancés. Ever. Got it?"

He stood still, watching her. A tiny muscle in his left

cheek twitched, the only sign of movement, but she read the silent message. He'd leave it, for now.

And wait for her to bring it up again. Which she wouldn't, so that was fine. Just fine.

She turned and strode away, choking back emotions she thought she'd dealt with, but facing Zach—recognizing the goodness in him—made her realize she could never erase enough of her family's past to consider a future with an honest cop like him. And she was surprised how much that hurt.

CHAPTER SIX

THE DECK DECAY HAD SPREAD to the opening of Zach's family room, and the realization made him long to punch someone. Or something.

The rotted boards meant water damage might extend into the family room wall. "Not good." Marty's observation spiked Zach's frustration level. It wasn't his father's fault that the two-week project would probably take twice as long, especially because he'd be returning to work in a few days. Gainful employment swallowed large chunks of time.

"Gotta tear it out. I'll help."

Zach hesitated. His father excelled at working with animals, farmland and big equipment. But he'd always avoided home repair whenever possible. Regardless, Zach couldn't refuse the offer. "There's not much room back here." As it was he was splayed on his belly, trying to wrench out pieces of decayed wood, inch by splintered inch.

"I'll start from this end," Marty decided. He peeled off his outer shirt and hunched down. "I grabbed an extra pry bar from McKinney's. Figured there must be a problem if this was taking you so long."

Zach hunted for censure in his father's tone, but found none. Had he been too sensitive to Marty's ways growing up? Too quick to take offense?

They worked steady, moving along the twenty-foot strip at a tortoise pace, but by mid-afternoon, they'd removed the bad piece. "Hand me that flashlight, would you, Dad?"

"This little thing?" Marty frowned as he handed it over. "What good can that... Oh." He stopped criticizing when the high-intensity LED light came on. "That's crazy bright. When did they come up with those things? While I was whacked out?"

"You were sick, Dad," Zach shot back, but he saw the grim look on his father's face and knew his father's term was factual. In layman's terms, Marty had been incorrigible, but he was better now. Which meant he was forced to face a host of changes. Thanks to Zach. "And yes, they're common now. And it looks like the next board up and the plywood are good from here. No rot."

"You need to buy the lumber to replace that piece we just chiseled out, don't you?"

"Yes."

"Then let's roll." Marty stood, swiped his hands to his pants and headed for the SUV. "Maybe we can grab a burger while we're out. The puppies are fed and I'm hungry. I expect you are, too."

Zach couldn't deny it. "Starved. I put off lunch because I didn't want to stop until we got to clean wood."

"Annoyingly thorough." Marty grunted as he settled into the passenger seat. "Your mother liked to say you got that from me."

Remembering his mother's easygoing ways, Zach couldn't refute her assessment. "Most likely."

He slid a quick glance his father's way, and thought he saw a flash of pride in the older man's face, but the look turned to a grimace when Marty inhaled deeply. "We don't smell too pretty."

Another fact Zach couldn't deny. "No one will care at the lumberyard."

"But we'll get our food to go," Marty decided. "I can't think anyone would appreciate being downwind of us about now. Still, it's a good job done. Now we're ready to move on."

"Yes." As he turned the truck toward Clearwater, Zach took another look Marty's way. His father looked satisfied for the first time since he'd brought him home. Pleased with himself. And Zach.

And that felt better than Zach ever thought it could.

"Don't you go back to work soon?" Marty faced Zach on Saturday, waiting as his mid-morning coffee brewed. "It's been over a week."

"Tuesday," Zach answered, leaning against the counter.

Marty stayed quiet, then looked the kitchen over with his gaze. "This waking up business…"

Zach's heart paused, mid-beat, unsure where his father's conversation might be headed.

"I don't know what to make of things."

Zach waited, patient, letting his father continue.

"A different place. A different life. Nothing I can look at and remember."

Guilt clutched Zach's gut. "I know, Dad."

Marty shook his head. "You don't. You can't know. No one can. But that's just the thing, I don't get it, either. How someone can make a big mistake like that and then shrug it off later as if, 'Oh well…mistakes happen.'"

Guilt mushroomed. "We thought—"

His father's frown turned into a scowl. "I'm not blaming you. Or your brother and sister. I'm talking about the doctors who made life-and-death decisions, decisions that changed my life. The whole family's. There's a part of me that wants to go back to that medical center and see what they have to say for themselves. How do they intend to fix this? But if I sue them for their ineptitude, what does that get me? A lot of aggravation while I pad some lawyer's bank account. But someone should pay, shouldn't they?" He leveraged his gaze to Zach, man-to-man. "Shouldn't someone, somewhere, take responsibility for messing up people's lives like this?"

"Now that you're feeling better, we can examine your options. Your insurance paid for the majority of the care you received while you were sick, so the proceeds from the sale of the farm are still in the bank."

"What am I gonna do? Start over? At my age? With no family, no kids to help, no one to step in and take over when I'm done? It's different when you start something like that when you're young. Young men have dreams." Marty shrugged that off. "What would be the point now?"

Zach drained his cup and set it in the sink. "There's always a point to doing what you love, isn't there?"

"Like police work?"

And there it was, a tiny stab because Zach was the third of three kids to walk away from the family farm. The last hope, the final link in a broken chain. "You gotta grow where God plants you. For me, it's the force. Protecting. Watching. Serving."

Marty stared out the back window. Piper's near paddock stood just beyond their property line, but Marty wasn't seeing the here and now. Zach knew that. He was remembering sprawling fields of green-cut hay. Thick alfalfa, rich and full. Hundreds of cows dotting the far pasture, young heifers waiting to be freshened, pastured to the left of the new barn. A pretty colonial farmhouse with a wraparound porch. Grandpa's house down the road, not far from the interstate. Huge tractors, mind-boggling equipment, an enterprise grown from three generations of frugality and hard work.

Gone.

Sold.

By Zach.

Remorse bit deep, but Marty wasn't looking for apologies. He wanted answers.

And payback.

But no amount of money could regain the history they'd lost nearly two years before. Regret speared deeper.

He could have taken a leave and run the farm for a little while. The hired help had been in place. He could have sacrificed a portion of his life to see. Just to see.

But it was too late now. He'd had the chance to make the sacrifice and chose otherwise.

Did Ethan jump in to take over? Or Julia? They were as schooled on the farm as you were.

But they had families. Careers.

So did you. You've worked hard to become an officer in the troop. You're up for promotion. And no one expected your father to get better.

Marty's prognosis had been life-alteringly grim: early-onset Alzheimer's, advancing at a rapid rate.

Only now he was fully functioning and there was nothing left to do. No farm. No house. No equipment, no cows.

"I'm heading next door to help Berto," Marty announced as he set his mug in the sink. "We're talking about how to make things run more efficiently. He's a good man. Piper is lucky to have him. You staying here?" Marty's glance took in Zach's clean jeans and shirt as if finding them wanting, because why would anyone be clean in the middle of the day?

"I'm taking Piper and the twins to the carnival."

"Ah."

His father almost smiled, and that made Zach feel better. "She wouldn't have said yes if you weren't here to help out. So, thank you."

"Those girls will love going on rides," Marty told him. "You were the only one who would go on the crazy, spinning rides. Ethan got sick easy and Julia would grab me like a spider monkey if I tried to take her on anything faster than the merry-go-round. But you?" His expression didn't reveal how he felt, but his voice pitched deeper. "You were always ready for something bigger. Bolder. Faster."

"We'll see which way the twins go," Zach told him as he moved to the door. "They've never been to the carnival before."

"Never?" Marty turned his attention back to the window, then paused, thinking. He followed Zach out the door, checked to make sure it locked behind him and fell into step alongside his son. "That's the problem with running a farm with no spouse. If I was busy, your mom could take you places. If she was busy, I could do the running around."

Zach couldn't remember more than a few times when his father did the running. He remembered Marty on a tractor, in the fields, in the barn, working, working, working.

Mom had been the chauffer, the taxi driver, the one with a list of who needed to be where and when. But if it made his father feel better to put a different spin on things, so be it. They parted ways at the corner of the near barn.

"Have fun." Marty looked beyond Zach. His expression changed. A soft look touched his father's face. "I'd say it's a lucky man that gets to escort three such lovely ladies to the carnival grounds."

Zach turned.

Dorrie and Sonya raced his way, their squeals contagious. Piper followed more slowly, and Zach decided then and there that he was clearly cut out to wear a detective's badge, because he'd deduced she'd look great in a dress at their first meeting.

Today proved it.

He sucked back a whistle of appreciation. The floral print dress with thin shoulder straps flowed over her figure. Copper-toned freckles dotted her shoulders, a shade that matched the cinnamon tone of her hair. Pale, translucent skin made her seem more vulnerable, but the look in her eye said she'd throw blue jeans on in a heartbeat if he wasn't careful.

He smiled, met her gaze and paused for long, slow seconds as the girls clamored for his attention. "Thank you."

"For …?" She raised a brow in question, but didn't try to shush the girls as she usually would. Her attention was solely on him, and that flattered his male ego.

"Wearing it."

A tiny smile started at her mouth and made its way to her cheeks, her eyes, a glimmer that seemed shy and flirtatious at once. "You asked."

"Yes."

She shrugged one pretty shoulder as if that was all it should ever take…. He would ask. She would comply, if possible.

He saw it then, plain as day, the spirit within the woman. Piper was a true-to-heart person, the kind who never played games, who strove to do good and be strong. A Martha mindset with a Mary heart in a crazy business that drained time like water down a creek.

He noted her shoulders with a look of concern. "Arent' you going to burn?"

"Sunscreen," she told him. "We slathered it on them too, but their skin just absorbs the sun. Mine?" She made a face of resignation. "No farmer's tan for me. Not with this skin."

He wanted to hold her hand, but he held back, and grabbed Dorrie's hand in one, then Sonya's in the other. "Ready?"

"Yes!" They answered in tandem. Piper took Sonya's

other hand and they moved down the driveway toward the road, not touching, but linked by the joy of a small child between them.

Piper flashed him a smile over Sonya's head, and that look made him wonder what her children would look like.

Copper-haired? Pale-skinned? A curly-haired girl or a buzzed-head boy?

"Thank you so much for bringing us, Trooper Zach." Dorrie peered up at him. She squeezed his big hand with her tinier one. "Grandma says we should be extra good, and I feel like being extra good today, so it should be easy, right?"

"Absolutely." He grinned down at her as she marched along, lilac ribbons bouncing with each step, her childlike innocence a blessing. He'd felt burdened a few minutes ago, pondering his father's change of circumstances. He knew they should celebrate Marty's recovery, and they would.

Right after they figured out how to give him back the life they'd stolen from him.

Sonya tugged his other arm. "I think they have cotton candy at this thing. Don't they?"

"We'll see." He matched her hopeful smile with one of his own, and pledged to put angst and worry behind him for the day. Right now, he wanted to show three girls the best summer afternoon he could muster. That would be enough for the moment.

"I thought this would be more difficult." Zach leaned close to Piper and spoke the words with quiet deliberation. "Coming to a busy carnival, keeping track of two kids who disappear on a regular basis. I rehearsed ways to find them in the crowd. I even brushed up on how to issue an Amber Alert if one of them went missing."

"I think that's awesome," Piper replied. She smoothed a hand across the full skirt of the sundress and pretended not to notice as his gaze followed the movement. "Our reality is quite different, though, and I can't say I mind."

"Seven merry-go-round rides later, I must agree." He laughed, reached over and squeezed her hand.

Then didn't let go.

Her pulse spiked.

She should move her hand from under his. Nudge him away. Or give him an elbow to the midsection. That would back him off.

But the truth was, she longed to move closer. Curl alongside that broad chest and muscled arm. See if he was lost in the moment. She certainly was.

"Can we go again?" Dorrie raced their way, eyes wide, excitement speeding her step.

"May we."

She huffed with impatience. "May we?"

Zach released Piper's hand and took Dorrie's instead. "Let's try those little airplanes. Okay?" He turned her toward the miniature biplanes across the center of the high school football field.

"You mean...fly?" Dorrie's eyes rounded.

"That's exactly what I mean," Zach told her. "Sonya. Let's try the other rides, okay?"

Sitting astride the horse she'd claimed seven rides earlier, she thrust out her lower lip. "I like this one."

"Oh, we get that." Piper exchanged a grin with Zach and moved toward the merry-go-round. "But we need to give other kids a chance on that horsey, right?"

"It's mine."

Piper decided against a battle in public. "Does he have a name?"

"It's a girl."

"Oh." Piper accepted that pronouncement easily. "Well. Does she have a name?"

"I can give her a name?" Sonya's countenance brightened. "For real?"

"Sure." Piper reached over and plucked her from the dark roan carousel pony while the girl's mind toyed with name possibilities. "How about Rosey?"

"That's a silly name for a horse."

The kid was right, so Piper tried harder. "Christabelle."

"Too long." Sonya paused, thinking, one finger tapping her chin. This, Piper knew, could go on for a very long time.

"What kind of horse is she?"

"Oh." Sonya caught on instantly. "Like in the book we have, right?"

"Exactly."

Sonya peered over her shoulder, then grasped Piper's hand as they made their way across the grass. "A Thoroughbred."

"A racehorse. Well. In that case," Piper made her face go prim and proper. "She should have a name that goes with a pedigree."

"Like our red cows."

"Exactly." Piper beamed, glad the little girl had been paying attention. "How about Lady Flora?"

"Oh. I like that name, Aunt Piper." Sonya trained her eyes on the hard plastic pony across the way. "Lady Flora the Thoroughbred."

"It's perfect." Zach joined the conversation as he double-checked Dorrie's seat belt in her white plane. "Would you like to ride with your sister, or pilot your own plane?"

"With her." Sonya pointed at Dorrie.

"I want to be by myself." Dorrie made a face at Sonya.

Sonya's lower lip popped out as if on cue. "But I don't like to do things alone."

Which is exactly why they were separating the girls that fall at school. One craved independence. The other one feared it. Time for a change. "You rode the pony by yourself," Piper counseled. "I think you'll be fine in the plane, Sonya."

Sonya clung closer to Piper's leg, if such a thing was possible. "It's not really a racehorse," she whispered. Her eyes implored Piper to understand the difference. "It's a horse on a spinning floor. But this—" she darted a quick glance to the small planes, fastened to a central turning gear by a long bar "—these really fly."

"I like flying." Zach tossed the information out like it was any old day.

Sonya didn't bite. "You're so big, Trooper Zach. And you're old. Of course you like it."

"Ouch." He pretended a shot to the heart, but then another voice weighed in from two planes down.

"She could ride with me." A girl about the twins' age patted the seat beside her. "If you want to."

Sonya looked at Dorrie.

Dorrie sat taut, face front, refusing eye contact, determined to stand her ground. Piper had been pushing for this very thing, more independence for both girls, but the current reality left Sonya high and dry.

Sonya turned, reluctant. "You're sure it's okay?"

"Yes." The other little girl sent them a small smile, a look that hinted at wisdom beyond her years. "I've been wanting to meet a friend. My name's Cat."

"That's a funny name."

"Sonya." Piper started to scold Sonya's honesty, but the other little girl smiled.

"It is, kind of, but my mother loved nature. So she named me Cactus. But everybody calls me Cat."

"Do you want to steer the plane?" Sonya wondered as she climbed aboard. "It's okay with me if you do."

"We both can," Cat replied. "And maybe we can go faster than your sister."

"I'd like that!"

Piper backed away quietly. Was this what school would be like for the girls? A series of quick successes? Or would it be day after day of trauma? She was praying for the former.

"Cat, we've got to go, honey." A dark-haired woman called Sonya's copilot after their third ride. "Your brother needs his nap."

"Okay." No fuss. No argument, wheedling or cajoling. Piper decided she needed to schedule a chat with the other woman, because Cat's behavior bordered on unbelievable. Every now and then, blind obedience would be a lovely change from constant battles.

Cat hopped out of the plane, but before she reached the access gate, she turned and met Sonya's gaze. "You did great," she told her in a voice that sounded too old for her years. "I'd ride with you anytime."

"Thanks. Me, too." A light of confidence sparked Sonya's face. She raised her chin. "And I can fly this plane all by myself, Aunt Piper."

"Glad to hear it." Piper reached an arm around Cat's thin shoulders and hugged her. "Thank you for riding with her."

"It was fun."

"I'm glad."

As the girl rounded the ticket booth, Zach noted the questioning look in Piper's eyes. "You know who she is, don't you?"

Piper shook her head. "No."

"She and her little brother came wandering out of the forest preserve last month. A couple of campers found them after that bad storm."

Piper's expression changed. "I remember. How could anyone forget that story?"

He nodded, grim. "They're in foster care, and the guys on the force make sure they've got everything they need. But the little guy…" Zach pulled a deep breath as he watched the trio move through the crowd of young families. "He's not doing too well. They don't..." He paused, worked his jaw, then shrugged one shoulder. "They don't expect him to make it."

Piper heard the note in his voice and read the look in his eye. "Oh, Zach."

Zach didn't forget his vow to maintain distance between him and Piper McKinney. He'd reminded himself multiple times a day in the last two weeks. But right now, she needed a hug.

His parents had lost a child at age three. His brother Cameron had died from leukemia before Zach was born. He'd never known his brother, and hadn't seen his parents' grief, but every holiday and holy day, his mother would stop by the hillside cemetery just north of I-86 and decorate Cam's grave. Ethan wouldn't go with her and Julia always made herself scarce, pretending she didn't know her mother's mission.

But Zach rode along because he saw the sadness in his mother's eyes and longed to chase it away.

Right now Piper needed a hug and Zach had one to give. When it came time to let go and step back, releasing her was the last thing he wanted to do.

Then Piper withdrew her phone from the narrow bag she had slung around her neck, read the time and grimaced.

The frown reenergized Zach's vow to keep his distance. Because he knew exactly what she was going to say before she said it. He knew because he was Marty Harrison's son, and his father always imposed time limits on having fun. He recognized the resignation on Piper's face, and remembered why he kept creating distance between them.

Because he'd been raised by a farmer who could never

let the day unfold without worry, and he'd vowed to never live that life again.

"Why are you guys back so soon?" Marty had been approaching the milking shed, but he veered their way instead. "Are the girls okay? Did someone get sick?"

Zach stayed quiet, because he was wondering the same thing. Why had they ended a delightful afternoon when the late-day milking was covered?

Marty faced Piper. "Did you think we couldn't handle this?"

She waved him off and moved toward the house. "I knew you could handle it just fine, but there's rain predicted for tomorrow and if I don't side-dress that corn, I may have wasted the only opportunity this hot summer will give me."

Marty took a cell phone from his pocket and waggled it. "Berto could have handled the corn. Or me."

The aggrieved look she shot him as she entered the house made him re-pocket the phone and bend lower, refocusing his attention on the twins. "Did you have fun, girls?"

"So much!" Sonya skip-danced in excitement, her side ponytail dangling lower than it had hours before. "Trooper Zach bought us cotton candy and chicken nuggets and ice cream and we rode on so many things and we met a new girl and saw the water and there were sailboats everywhere."

Marty's smile said he enjoyed the play-by-play. "Perfect day for sailing. Not much wind, but enough of a light breeze. And that's one thing I really like about being here."

Zach turned, surprised. His father hadn't found much to his liking since the surgery that removed pressure on his brain from accumulated fluids and returned him to good health.

"That view." Marty gazed down the hill and over the road, where the northwest end of the lake stretched before them. The village trees blocked most of the buildings, but a stretch of Water Street banked left through a small clearing. Old-style homes dotted the road. A church spire rose from just beyond the homes. A rectangular opening framed the old brass bell, and a metal cross sparkled rays of light in the afternoon sun. Distant trees framed the church, the homes, the winding street that gave way to boat slips and docks leading into the water.

"They have a 'ring of fire' on the Fourth of July," Zach told him.

Marty frowned, not understanding.

"Everybody makes a campfire along the shore," Dorrie explained. "And when you go down there to make your fire, it gets dark and everybody can see all the fires, all around the lake. It is so beautiful, Mr. Marty."

"Sounds like it would be."

"And I think our fire was the best of all," Sonya told him. "Berto made sure we used the best dry wood, and he knows how to make the fire look really big. Piper said it was the best campfire ever."

"And we toasted marshmallows," Dorrie added.

"And hot dogs." Sonya wasn't about to be outdone.

"And Sonya puked."

"I did not!" Sonya wasn't about to let that go unchallenged. "I *almost* puked and that's a big difference."

"Aunt Piper told Grandma you threw up on the way home." Dorrie rolled her eyes as if throwing up was childish. "Aunt Piper wouldn't lie about that."

"On the way home doesn't count," Sonya countered smoothly. "It only counts if it happens at the lake. And it didn't. So there."

"Sonya! Doralia! We must feed your goat, no?"

"We can tell Beansy about the carnival!" Dorrie spun and high-fived her twin.

Sonya raced ahead, her angst forgotten. "He'll love hearing about the plane rides!"

"And they're off." Zach couldn't help but laugh at their quick turnabout. His father's look said he was familiar with that part of childhood.

Piper came out of the house behind Lucia. She'd cut off the arms of the T-shirt she'd donned, and her upper arms looked good. They were strong enough to fix tractors but soft enough to comfort a small child's fears in the night.

She was a package, all right, but Zach knew his limits. He turned back to his father. "Do the pups need feeding?"

Marty nodded. "If you don't mind. I made up enough formula to last through tomorrow morning. Mom always said fresh was better for tiny tummies."

Zach smiled. It sounded like something his mother would say. "I'll take care of the pups while you do the milking. And Dad?"

Marty turned, puzzled.

"Thanks for today." Zach directed a look toward Piper, then beyond, where the girls' chatter could be heard. "We had a great time."

The hinted smile he thought he'd seen that morning made an encore appearance, tiny and unpracticed, but there. Marty's gaze flicked back to the lake, then to his son. "My pleasure."

Zach headed out, avoiding Piper on purpose.

They'd had fun. A beautiful afternoon he hoped the twins would remember for a long time to come. And that's how they'd leave it, because he read the work-first timeline in Piper's face, in her actions. Nothing got in the way of the success of the farm.

So be it. Her life, her choice.

He'd deliberately chosen differently, and he refused to tackle that life again. Not now. Not ever. He'd been silly to think he'd misread the signs that she might be able to put aside work for family time.

Now he knew better. In two days he'd be reporting back to work, and they'd go back to being neighbors with a property line in common.

And that was all they'd be.

CHAPTER SEVEN

Y OU CUT THEIR DAY SHORT for nothing. You get
that, right?

Piper mentally chastised herself as she checked the
activity at the dairy store on Sunday afternoon, a dry,
hot, no-rain-in-sight kind of day. That meant her hurry
to fertilize the corn fields the previous night was a waste
of time.

The languid, lazy day tempted families to stop in for
a mid-afternoon treat. Some walked up from the town.
Some drove. Some came by after church, gathering fresh
milk, eggs and bread for their day of rest.

Piper scowled at the western sky.

Blue. Bright. Sunny. The bank of clouds forming over
Lake Erie pushed north, away from Kirkwood Lake.

And despite her mini panic attack about missing a
God-given opportunity to side-dress the corn, the twins
sang her praises. They thanked her repeatedly, retelling
stories of grand horses, flying machines and melt-in-
your-mouth cotton candy. Pink for Sonya. Yellow for
Dorrie.

She'd noted Zach's expression yesterday. Saw the
disappointment. He wanted to stay, prolong the girls' fun.

She'd opted to work.

She strode across the browning grass, disenchanted
with herself, with life and maybe with farming. For a

few short hours she'd let herself relax on the enjoyable afternoon. Chill out. Have fun.

Colin's words came back to her, the Realtor's offer dangling like a gold ring at the county fair.

She could choose "easy". Seven figures, even split five ways, was a sizable opportunity. Was God tempting her? Maybe opening doors she'd closed out of stubbornness?

"Piper?"

Zach's voice hailed her.

He'd walked away yesterday, shoulders back, chin up, and she read that posture like the open pages of large-print book.

She'd been given the cold shoulder.

So be it. She was pretty sure a lecture would be forthcoming, but a crew of small voices surprised her.

"Mom, can we get ice cream? Please?"

"I would wike some, Uncle Zach. A wot."

One little boy tugged Zach's hand in the direction of the ice cream windows. Another little fellow snuggled into his mother's side, curled against her chest, his dark mop of curls a longer version of Zach's hair. He eyed "Uncle Zach" from his cozy perch, begging in a softer voice.

Absolutely endearing. Both of them. And the woman at Zach's side looked like a feminine version of Marty.

"Piper, this is my sister, Julia. And her boys, Martin and Connor."

"Hey." Piper reached out a hand to Julia. "Welcome to Kirkwood Lake. Are you here to visit?"

"We are." Julia smiled up at Zach, but something in her face told Piper there was more to the story. "We're going to stay at Zach's place for a couple of weeks, and he wanted to introduce us."

They came to visit when Zach's vacation was drawing to an end?

Piper stowed that odd bit of information for examination later. "Well, it's a pleasure. And your boys are beautiful."

"They're monsters, but we like 'em." Julia grinned at the smaller boy and he flashed her a wide smile, full of love and trust. But he didn't loosen his grip as his eyes took in the big barns, lowing cattle, calf pens and laughter of children near the ice cream windows.

"I thought the girls might get a kick out of playing with the boys while they're here." Zach palmed the bigger boy's head. "Martin's their age and they can all take turns torturing Connor."

"Yes!" Martin fist-pumped the air, delighted by the prospect.

Connor frowned down at his brother and burrowed closer into Julia's shoulder.

"Kidding, little guy." Zach put a reassuring hand on the toddler's back. Connor peeked up, smiled and held out his arms.

Zach gathered him in, then swung the tiny fellow up to his shoulders. Connor shrieked, and for a moment looked as though he'd go into full-fledged meltdown.

But then the little guy's face brightened. Eyes wide, he crowed when Zach moved, but the little eek! turned into a joyous laugh.

He was safe and secure. On top of the world. A little precarious, but trusting his uncle to keep him safe.

Seeing Zach with Julia, playing with her sons, made Piper long for that picture of family love. Why couldn't her family be like that? Strong in faith and love?

"We're grilling tonight." Julia turned toward Piper and indicated Zach's place with a glance. "Why don't you guys come over? Zach said they've bummed a bunch of meals off you in the past couple of weeks. And unlike my little brother here—" she aimed a look of loving appreciation Zach's way "—I'm a great cook."

"Although I'll be the one grilling," Zach added.

Piper raised her gaze to Zach's. He smiled, but it wasn't the warm, engaging grin she'd come to know. It was pleasant, a pale image of his normal self. "Umm…"

"Dad's coming over for the afternoon milking." Zach offered the information in a calm voice. Cool. Deliberate. As if talking to any old neighbor. Funny how that pinched her ego.

"With Julia here he doesn't have to do that. Berto and I can manage."

"He wants to," Julia told her. "And that's okay. The boys and I will be there when the chores are done. Dad always loved chore time. Remember, Zach?" A hint of melancholy shadowed her soft smile. "He'd whistle his way through Handel's Hallelujah Chorus while milking. Or Beethoven's 'Ode to Joy.' He always said it was the best time to pray, while he was outside, working with the animals."

"It is." Piper decided her barn work could be put on hold for a few minutes. She turned toward the ice cream windows. "Is it okay if we treat the boys?"

"No." Zach's answer surprised her, but it shouldn't have. His reaction yesterday said he wanted to keep his distance. A good thing for both, she decided, but she realized distance wasn't what she wanted when she looked into those bright blue eyes.

"We'll pay for our ice cream and ensure your bottom line." He shot her a smile, more genuine this time, and moved ahead.

She wished he wasn't so nice.

She wished he liked farming.

She wished he wasn't a cop.

Suddenly the developer's offer came to mind.

Money. Free and clear. No debt. A fresh beginning, a new tomorrow.

"Did you see my Grandpa's puppies?" Martin pointed to Zach's house across the back field. "They're so cute!"

"They are. I got to help feed them the other night."

"Really?" Martin's eyebrows shot up. "Grandpa says I can't feed them until they're bigger but I'm only going to be here for a couple of weeks. Or maybe until my daddy moves back to our house."

Silence reigned.

Zach stopped dead in his tracks. He made eye contact with his sister, then swallowed hard. Piper stood still, too, but then realization hit. This was nothing they'd want to talk about in front of the boys. "My dad had to go here and there, too," she told Martin. Five years old was too young to have to deal with crazy adult drama, but Piper was no stranger to that, so she squatted until she was eye-level with the boy. "He was working on all sorts of things, and there were times when he'd pack up and go off for days. And we just kept busy until we saw him again."

"Then that's what we'll do," Martin decided. "Right, Mom? We'll just keep busy."

"You've come to the right place for that," Zach told the boys. He sent his sister a gentle look, so filled with compassion that Piper's eyes grew damp. "Farms are busy places."

"And there's the lake." Piper pointed down the hill. "We have a small boat that's great for fishing. And for trolling around, checking out the water."

"I didn't know that." Zach's voice drew her attention as they took their place in line at the first window. "You have a boat?"

Piper shrugged. "My brothers aren't big on fishing and I'm short on time."

She didn't look up, purposely. She didn't want to see the disappointment on his face. And it was pretty silly to live on a lake, have a boat and never go out on the water. "Why don't you use it to take the boys out while they're here?"

"I go back to work on Tuesday, so I can take them

fishing for a little while tomorrow," Zach decided. "Did you ever eat lake perch, Piper?"

"I love lake perch," she admitted. "My dad used to catch them by the buckets. I even helped fillet them, but I probably shouldn't admit that."

"Because the minute you admit to knowing something, someone expects you to do it," Julia added.

"Exactly." Piper smiled at her.

Noreen leaned out the ice cream window to admire the boys. "Noreen, this one's on us," Piper said.

"I thought I nixed that idea." Zach aimed a no-nonsense gaze her way, but Piper waved him off.

"Gotta welcome our summer visitors in style. I must get back to work, but you should have them meet the twins. And Beansy. Lucia's in the house with the girls."

"You're not having ice cream with us?" Zach's voice held a note of question. "But supper is a yes, right?"

It shouldn't be a yes. Piper knew that. But Marty and Zach had been good to them, and refusing to let them feed her family would be rude. "What time?"

"Let's eat late so you can get stuff done. Seven-thirty okay? And I'm making a campfire for the kids."

Dorrie and Sonya would love that. "We'll be there. Julia." Piper turned and offered Zach's sister a broad smile. "Nice to meet you. And your boys."

"Thank you, Piper."

Their exchanged look left a lot unstated, but Piper understood what happened to family when there was a breakup. Kids were part of the collateral damage. No matter what else happened in her life, she craved a happily ever after with her one true love.

But she'd been surrounded by the opposite, so maybe that was *her* collateral damage: a wounded heart seeking a perfect tomorrow.

She headed to the back pasture to screen the heifers. Some were due to calve, some were ready to be bred and others were lolling, not quite ready to join the healthy dairy herd she'd developed over a decade.

Brown grass crunched beneath the tires of her aging pickup truck. Stunted corn swayed on Vince and Linda's knoll, up the hill. What should be lush appeared yellowed, even from this distance.

Water.

The corn needed water, and without God-given rain, there'd be none. Bad drought was a rarity in the northern Appalachians, but this year it reared its head.

They'd survived dry years before. And wet ones. Wet ones were worse, in fact, so she'd deal with it and move forward, day by day. She had Lucia, Berto and the girls relying on her, depending on the farm. One way or another, she'd make it work.

"No one does half-chickens over a wood fire like this anymore. And I don't remember this fire pit being here, but I can't imagine when you've had time to build it with the work you're putting in on that deck. It's gorgeous, by the way. I love how the fieldstone here complements the stone of the house." Piper took a breath and inhaled the mouthwatering scent of grilling chicken, as Lucia and Julia watched the kids zipping across a hose-fed lawn mat.

"And once again she manages multiple sentences before pausing to breathe." Zach sounded wry, but his easy look gentled her heart. Calmed her spirit. "The fire pit came as a kit that I found at Home Depot last week when Dad and I had to make a tool run. Dad worked on it between milking, tractors and puppies."

"Not much of a vacation for a guy who doesn't want to be married to his work," Piper noted, sinking onto one of the benches drawn up near the fire pit, but far enough back to avoid the heat. "Shouldn't a vacation be restful?"

"I think helpful outweighs restful most often." Zach adjusted the height of his grill with a clever turning device he'd mounted next to the fire pit. "My father loves helping on the farm. The puppies are thriving—"

"Can I see them?"

Her eagerness earned her the first full-fledged smile she'd seen him flash since yesterday afternoon. "Once the water wars are over." He lifted his gaze to the Slip'N Slide area. "Otherwise we'll have soaking wet kids wanting to tromp in with you. And Dad's moving the pups to an outside pen in the shade of the garage tomorrow."

"Smelly." She made a face up at him and laughed when he nodded.

"Yes. They're big enough now and it's plenty warm enough, so if you hear yipping and yapping, please don't call animal control on me for disturbing the peace."

"I won't, but only because you've stopped complaining about my roosters. Except, I expect they'll annoy you again once you're back at work. And then we're back to square one."

"Are we?" The look he aimed her way said he wasn't so sure. "I think we passed square one but hit a fork in the road, and neither one of us knows which path to take."

"The road less traveled." Piper drew her knees up and locked her hands around them. "Robert Frost lived on a farm. Did you know that?"

Zach tipped a lazy grin her way, turning her tough-girl will to putty. "Is that supposed to make me like farming more? Because it doesn't. And his first farm was a dismal failure. Bet you didn't know that or you wouldn't be spewing your poetry facts quite so freely."

"I didn't, but it makes little difference if he kept his eye on the goal and eventually became a successful poet and farmer. I think his story is meant to open our eyes to the possibilities around us," she returned. "And you can't hate farming as much as you make out or you wouldn't have bought a house bordering a farm."

"I like fishing. Hunting. Living in the country." Zach reached out long-handled tongs to turn the sizzling meat. "And I must admit, I kind of enjoyed helping you out the past couple of weeks. Now and again." He quirked a grin her way. "Probably because it was the exception, not the rule."

"I hear ya." She contemplated the fire, then the farm. A stray wind rose up. It wasn't strong, but enough to fan the flames. The random breeze made Zach readjust the height of his grilling plate and force Piper to push her hair back, behind her ears. "I wonder what makes us love things. Or dislike them. Is the affinity for a certain profession the same as having a talent? Like painting or drawing? Or is it because the odd tumblers of fate push you in one direction or another?"

"God. And fate."

Piper frowned. "I don't think it can be both, Zach."

He laughed. "Sure it can. You're born with God-given talent."

She nodded agreement.

"But life hands you an array of experiences, good and bad. So you're made up of those experiences. We're like baseballs," he noted, eyes down, keeping the flames in check.

"Baseballs."

"You're laughing at me, but it's a good analogy," he continued as he studied the meat, watching for bursts of flame as chicken fat tempted the heat to ignite. "The core of the ball is firm and hard. But the ball won't move properly through the air without the bands surrounding that core. And each band is slightly different, made of different yarns. Different thicknesses."

"Like our experiences."

"Yes. But then each ball is hand-stitched and that's like God, molding us and shaping us. Tugging us in one direction or another, if we're smart enough to follow his lead."

"So God led you away from the farm?" With the Realtor's current interest in McKinney Farm, Piper asked the question sincerely.

Zach shook his head. "No, I'm going to blame that one on good old-fashioned stubbornness."

Piper understood that. She'd dug her heels in a lot lately.

"The problem is," Zach continued, "if I'd known what was going to happen ten years later, I might have made different choices. But no one has that vantage point except God, so we make do with our choices and move on." He aimed a smile at his father across the yard. As Marty moved their way, Zach dropped his tone. "Let's curtail this discussion for a bit, okay? Dad's heading this way."

"Gotcha."

Marty had been very good to her and the farm these past two weeks. If continuing a conversation about leaving a farm would hurt the older Harrison, she was okay leaving it alone for now. But a bevy of questions made her wonder about the whys and wherefores of Marty Harrison's farm. Still, it wasn't her business, not really. And his help was an absolute blessing, nothing to be taken lightly.

"I've got a proposition for you, Piper." Marty took a seat next to her, leaned forward, clasped his hands and then indicated her barns with a glance. "I'd like to start painting the outbuildings for you."

Piper followed the direction of his gaze and shook her head instantly. "I can't let you do that, Marty. It's too much, and I don't have money to pay you to help like that."

"Not lookin' for money. Don't need money. But you're

a farm girl and you know that a good roof and sound wood are crucial to a building."

"Yes. But—"

"We're at the lull time of the year right now. First hay is in. Winter wheat crop is still a few weeks out. And nothing after that but spreading manure and milking while we let Mother Nature and God manage the growing part of the season."

His words made sense, but painting big buildings was a huge project. Still, the offer tempted her. But it would be wrong to put Marty to work like that. "Marty, you've got Julia here. And the boys."

"I'll manage time for both. The way I see it, if we can get one full barn done this year, we can tackle the ell of the other barn next year."

It did make sense. Piper turned toward Zach, but he studied the grill, silent. "I..."

"Good!" Marty clapped his hands and stood, laughing down at her. "You know years ago, when I was probably Zach's age, a couple of young fellas came by my place, looking for work. They didn't want pay, they were doing country mission work, they said. They went from town to town, offering their help to farmers and talking about faith." He directed his gaze toward McKinney Farm and then back to Piper. "Consider me your country mission help. It makes me feel good to walk down that center row of the milking parlor, watching those cows chew their cud. Mixing feed. Painting barns. You're helping me by letting me help you."

His words piqued Piper's curiosity. Why did Marty need help? Was there something she should know?

"I'll grab the paint tomorrow, and I won't take no for an answer. This is my way of saying thank you."

"For letting you work?" Piper didn't hide her disbelief. "You understand that's not how this usually works, right?"

"In this case, it's fine," laughed Marty. He stretched his

arms up, above his head, inhaled and then gave Zach a solid look of approval. "That smells really good."

"Ten minutes," advised Zach. "Can you have Julia get the kids dried off?"

"I'm on it." Marty strode off, looking stronger and younger than when Piper first met him two weeks before.

She turned to pepper Zach with questions but his face silenced her. He followed his father's progress with such a look of guilt and sadness that her heart longed to soothe them away.

She'd save her questions for later, when Marty wasn't around. She'd ask them eventually. She needed to, to find out the Harrison history. A part of her felt guilty for accepting their help with no payment, but Marty's story of those two wandering mission boys, back in the day...

God understood farmers. He understood sowers of seed; He'd used them in multiple parables. But He also blessed the family, the home, the heart of the farm, and asked His people to rest on the seventh day.

She never rested. Which meant she picked which commands to respect. Was she right? Wrong?

She wasn't sure, but she needed to do an examination of conscience more thoroughly than she had in a long time. Marty's willingness to work meant she should have more time. Instead, she kept thinking of more things she could get done because she had more time. That probably wasn't exactly what God had in mind.

"Piper, can you get me a platter from inside?"

"Sure." She stood, watching Zach reposition the chicken pieces to cook them evenly. He put care and caution into his grilling, his bed of coals just so.

"You're staring." He angled a slow smile her way, a smile that said he enjoyed being appreciated.

"I'm noting your cooking prowess. Nothing more." It wasn't full truth, but she was admiring his skills. And his hands, strong and dexterous. His profile, firm and ridged from brow to chin. The little dimple in his right cheek that flashed when he grinned. Like now.

"It's only one of my many attributes, but thank you. And that doesn't mean you can plunk me on some bicentennial committee for next year, flipping burgers and sausages at the fair. We'll have enough to do with crowd control."

"Is Marty as good with a grill?"

Zach's expression said Marty didn't come close. "He holds his own with burgers and hot dogs. And that's the first time he mentioned being here next year." Zach's words went back to the prior conversation. "We've been wondering what his plans were. He's not exactly the talkative type."

"I gathered that. And I take it he's not sure what to do now that he lost his farm."

Zach's face darkened. "Let's just say he's got time to decide. I pray about it. About him. The whole thing."

Curiosity pulled Piper forward, but Zach waved her off. "We'll discuss it sometime soon, but right now I need that platter. If you don't mind?" His expression said he didn't mind her inquisitiveness, but now wasn't the time or place.

"Be right back."

"Thanks, Piper."

She smiled back at him, over her shoulder, and the sight of him alongside the raised pit, manning the grilling area with masculine intent, made her appreciate him.

Yes, he was a cop. But he wasn't Hunter, and he proved that every single day.

He didn't like farming.

Still, with the Realtor's offer on the table, would she actually be farming in another year? If Vince and Linda's land sold, how would she manage enough acreage to make a profit? And should she sell now while she maintained the upper hand? Once the deal was done on

Vince's land, Piper would have to travel much farther to rent arable land. And that trip with huge equipment meant a loss of profits.

Confusion and insecurity wrangled in her thoughts as she entered the kitchen. A large, oval platter sat on the table, plain white stoneware. She picked it up and took it outside.

"Ah, thanks." Zach accepted the platter, set it down and began lifting the half-chickens.

"Great platter. It's huge. And heavy."

His smile said he agreed. "It was my mother's. We used it every Thanksgiving and Christmas for the roasted turkey."

"How nice."

"That woman could cook up a storm," he told her as he turned one piece of chicken a last time. "She helped on the farm when she needed to, but her talent was raising kids. Running the house. Raising the puppies. Chauffeuring people here and there. Keeping schedules straight. And keeping the books for Dad."

Piper took a step back to allow him room to hoist the platter. "You miss her."

"Every day." He sighed, then smiled. "But I believe we'll be together again. With my brother Cameron. He died before I was born and a part of my mom never stopped missing him."

The pure light of Zach's heart shone through his words, his understanding of his mother's loss. "And I bet your father worked through it differently."

"Or not at all." Zach waited while she slid the wide glass door to the family room open. "He's not a talker, he's a doer, so you might be right. But on the days when Mom went to Cam's gravesite—his birthday and holidays—Dad didn't go with her. I did."

Empathetic. Caring. Kind. Loyal and faithful to a fault. God had created this wonderful man and each quality made him more attractive. He set the meat down and turned her way. "I'm sorry. I shouldn't be talking about sad stuff on such a nice summer day. It's just that seeing Cat and her little brother yesterday—"

She nodded, remembering.

"Put me in mind of Cameron. And how my parents must have felt, tending him while he was sick and knowing he wasn't going to make it. I can't imagine being that strong."

She couldn't help herself. She reached up a hand to his face, his late-day bristle tickling her palm. "You're already that strong. I see it in the little things you do. The things you say. The care you give to those around you. So don't sell yourself short, Zach Harrison."

He reached up. Covered her hand with his, and the sight of his big, broad hand swallowing hers made her feel warm and protected. He grasped her hand, brought her palm to his lips and kissed it gently, a simple kiss that shouldn't have rocked her world, but did. The pressure of his hand…the feel of his lips against her skin…the sight of him, kissing her hand, then lifting the hand back to his cheek.

She melted, there on the spot.

"Oh, that smells so good!" The twins burst in, chattering a mile a minute. Martin followed, scrambling to be first in line. Damp-haired, clean and noisy, the kids clamored while Piper and Lucia helped fill their plates. Julia set them up at the picnic table under a wide, shady maple tree, then laughed when Connor eyed the group and padded back to the door.

"Smart kid." Zach noted. He eyed the three five-year-olds and lifted Connor up. "You eat in here with us, bud, because there's no telling what those three might think up. And you're not exactly ready for prime time when it comes to the playground set, are you?"

Connor shook his head. He might not understand exactly what his uncle said, but he was smart enough to recognize a rescue when he saw one. And Uncle Zach had just saved the day.

Zach tucked him into a booster seat, ignored the boy's protests and pointed down. "My chairs are high, and I prefer that we don't spend the evening in the ER. Therefore you sit in this seat and deal with it."

Connor eyed his options, but the food must have smelled too good. He sent a shy smile up to Zach. "'Kay."

"Nice job." Julia sent Zach a smile of gratitude as she filled her plate. "I'm impressed."

Lucia, Berto and Marty took their plates outside to the picnic table. Zach followed.

Piper stayed inside with Julia. When Julia tried to wave her out, Piper laughed out loud. "I spend my life outside, Julia. It's really a pleasure to sit in here. Eat in peace and quiet. No flies, bees or ants competing with me for my food."

"I can't argue that." Julia sank into the seat, smiled and sighed. "I wasn't sure what to expect when we got here." She indicated her father and brother with her gaze. "What we'd be walking into, but I have to say things are better than I imagined."

Piper drew her shoulders up. "I haven't got a clue what you're talking about, but your father and brother have been a big help to me."

"It's actually the other way around." Julia cut a clutch of grapes in half for Connor's plate. "But no matter how it happened, I'm so grateful that Zach bought this place, right next to yours. It's a godsend, Piper."

"But why, Julia? Why is working on a farm so good for your father, when he had a farm, lost it, but claims to have plenty of money? Because that scenario isn't exactly the norm, if you know what I mean."

"Zach hasn't told you about Dad?"

Concern snaked a path up Piper's spine. Hadn't she suspected there was more to this story? "What's to tell?"

"There's a fine line between invading someone's privacy and offering up full disclosure." Julia's face showed she was being pulled in two directions. "I'll let Zach tell you because he's the one who's had to deal with everything. And that makes me feel guilty, as if I haven't been around to do my share."

"You're here now. And that's nice for your dad, right?"

"And us." Julia pushed a little food around on her plate, but didn't eat. "I'm not sure what's going to happen right now, in my life. My marriage. And I know that was uncomfortable when Martin blurted out his father's absence yesterday."

"It made things awkward for you," Piper told her. "I'm sorry about that, but marriage isn't an easy business. Especially when times get tough."

"Or when your husband's student teacher is a size four sporting stiletto heels."

Piper hoped her face reflected her feelings. "That stinks."

Julia reached over to wipe a little barbecue sauce from Connor's chin and shrugged. "I'm not the kind of woman who sits back and smiles while her husband cheats on her. Right or wrong, we're here, for however long it takes to figure things out. I'm looking into jobs in the area. I'm a practicing midwife affiliated with an obstetrical practice in Ithaca, so I'm state-licensed. But maybe it's time for a full move, away from Central New York."

"Making new memories." Piper quoted Zach to his sister.

"And taking the time to sort through things. The good. And the bad."

Piper understood how hard that was, but the set of Julia's chin said she was determined to put things right. And not waste a whole lot of time doing it.

That was a quality Piper admired, especially now when she felt as if she were second-guessing herself every minute of every day.

Plan your work. Work your plan.

That was her father's simple work ethic. And it would have worked if her mother hadn't left with nearly a quarter-million of the farm's value in her bank account.

All hard work brings profit, but mere talk will bring only poverty.

The ancient Proverb rang true to Piper. Life shouldn't be *all* about work, but no one should be ashamed of a strong work ethic. Didn't the work of human hands settle this great country? Didn't the pioneers face great odds and prevail?

"Piper?" Lucia's voice called softly from the patio door. Piper turned.

Dorrie lay sound asleep in Lucia's arms, and from the look of Sonya, she wasn't far behind.

"We're going to take the girls home to bed." Lucia pointed her chin toward her brother. "I will see you at home."

"All right."

"They're so precious," Julia whispered the words as Lucia eased across the yard. "And so beautiful."

"And full of mischief, so don't let their appearances fool you." Piper smiled at the retreating figures, Berto and Lucia, both short and somewhat stocky but so dear to her heart.

The girls had no mother.

Piper had no mother.

But they shared Lucia and Berto, and Piper blessed the day the Hispanic family crept quietly into their lives, migrant workers picking a neighboring farmer's orchards.

"I've learned to count my blessings, Julia." She turned toward Zach's sister as she took her plate to the sink to be rinsed. "There's only so much we can control. And way more that we can't. But faith and family will see us through."

Julia sent her a smile of agreement, then lifted her tired little boy out of his booster seat. "I'm going to wash him up and get him ready for bed. Piper?"

Piper turned. "Hmm?"

"I'm so glad you're here."

She turned and walked to the stairs leading to the bedroom level of Zach's house.

Her words made Piper smile. She hadn't worked to keep her friendships as solid as she should. But seeing the twins with Martin and Connor, she realized she needed to do that. For their sake and hers. Because friends were a wonderful thing to have.

CHAPTER EIGHT

"**I**'LL WALK YOU HOME."

Zach had been waiting for Piper to come out of the house, watching the fire's glow while listening for the telltale click of the latch.

"I'll keep an eye on the fire," Marty announced to no one in particular.

Zach glanced his way, but the evening shadows didn't reveal a smile or a frown, just an angle of silhouette cutting across his father's face, like sun through a late-day window. "Thanks, Dad."

"It's a two-minute walk across the yard, through the field and around the barn." Piper whispered the words, half-scolding, as she set off. "And it's not even dark."

"Maybe I'm not walking you home to protect you. Maybe I just like walking you home."

"Oh."

He'd silenced her, a good trick, because Piper didn't do quiet easily. So he figured it was a good time to reach for her hand. Feel the texture of her palm against his fingers, the work-roughened skin different from any girl he'd dated before.

You're not dating Piper. We've discussed this. Too many red flags.

But he wanted to date Piper, he decided, so he shushed

the internal scolding and jumped into uncharted water. "Let's go out tomorrow night."

"Out? As in…out?"

"As in you. Me. A date."

Piper stepped up the pace as if anxious to get away. "As in: no."

He laughed, tugged her closer because he wasn't eager to have her escape, then kept her there while they walked. "Despite your animosity toward cops…"

"And yours regarding farms."

Zach acknowledged that with an easy shrug. "I think we need to test the waters. I haven't taken a pretty girl out in way too long, and the only one I seriously want to take out at the moment is you. You should go, because it would make me happy. And it's the night before I go back to work."

"What does that have to do with anything?" She stopped, halting their progress.

Fading pink rays cast an ethereal sheen on her skin, her hair, turning the copper brighter. Bolder.

Her face tipped in question, but it wasn't the verbal question he wanted to answer. It was the one that wondered what it would be like to kiss Piper. Hold her. Comfort her, laugh with her. When she wasn't all steamed up over something.

And maybe when she was.

That image made him smile as he leaned down. He slipped one arm behind her shoulders. The other one held her hand, so he looped their arms collectively around her, gently drawing her in, allowing her time to back away.

She didn't back away.

She stepped closer.

That was all the permission he needed. He kissed her, urging his lips to get to know hers, letting them wander her face, her hair, the scent of her, soap-and-water clean.

She kissed him back, despite her misgivings, as if kissing him had been on her mind for days. Or weeks. As it had been on his.

And when he was done, he wrapped her in a big hug, a hug that offered safety and warmth, an embrace that promised protection. When she laid her head against his heart, the cop in him noted the contradictions. Fast pulse and slow, steady breathing, as if she felt safe and secure in the loop of his arms. Right then he knew he was in over his head.

A cow bellowed from the back barn. Another followed suit. Then all went quiet except for the occasional frog call. Lightning bugs lit the air as the sun disappeared, tiny points of luminescence, a reminder of summers gone and summers yet to come.

"Well."

He leaned back and tipped her chin up. "That's all you've got to say?"

Her smile drew him to kiss her again, lightly. Sweetly. She sighed, and the sigh about did him in. If he hadn't fallen before, that soft sigh was enough to push him over the edge despite his concerns.

Was he putting himself in a bad position? Was he jumping back into a situation he'd worked so hard to get out of a decade ago? Was this God's idea of a joke?

"That was by far the nicest kiss I've ever had in my entire life."

Her honesty inspired his grin. "Good."

"Even though…"

"…we have issues we need to deal with." He finished the sentence for her. "But I think kisses like this—" he released her hand and cupped her cheek, marveling at the rose-petal softness as he leaned in for one more kiss, a kiss that made him yearn for more time "—go a long way toward compromise. Don't you agree?"

Her freckles faded in the dim light, but the pale ivory

beneath them made her look like an old-world painting in the deepening shadows. "I'm feeling more cooperative by the minute."

He laughed and re-grasped her hand. "So tomorrow night. A date. You. Me. No kids. Deal?"

"Yes."

"Good." He walked her to the back door, raised her hand as they climbed the steps, then offered a courtly bow. "It was my pleasure to escort you, my lady."

His gesture touched her. He saw it in her face, in the relaxed curve of her chin, in the little sigh that said romance and women made a good pairing. He was pretty sure Piper hadn't had time—or taken time—for much romance in her life.

He wanted to change that.

"Thank you, Zach."

"Six thirty tomorrow evening. I'll pick you up."

"I could walk over."

He frowned. "Definition of a date. Boy meets girl. Boy picks girl up. Boy shows girl a good time because he thinks girl is special. Got it?"

She laughed, sweet and carefree, and he realized she didn't laugh like that often. Was it the farm that held her back? Her family history?

Regardless, it was time to get to know Piper better. Yes, he could list the reasons why dating each other wasn't a good idea, but what if it turned out to be the best idea ever? How would they know if they kept skating around the attraction?

He leaned down and gave her one last kiss on the cheek, a soft kiss that let his mouth wander the sensitive skin there. Just a little. Enough to say he thought she was wonderful and special. "Good night."

"'Night. And thank you for supper. It was the best chicken I've ever had."

He grinned. "Well, if that's all I had to do to break down your defenses, I'd have barbecued sooner."

She retreated into the house, smiling, and seeing that smile, the spring to her step, made him feel good. He didn't know what would happen with her farm. He understood fractured family dynamics better than most, but he also recognized her dogged tenacity. She wouldn't go down without a fight.

He'd withhold judgment until he knew more. Marty had shared a few concerns, and no one understood the inner workings of a successful farming enterprise better than his father.

For right now, he had a date with a beautiful woman, a woman who made him smile and think hard at the same time. And maybe, just maybe, allow him to dream of what could be.

Julia was curled up in the wide recliner when he got back to the house. She smiled, raised the book in her hand and said, "I started this book three months ago. This is the first chance I've had to get back to it."

Zach sat across from her, leaned in and folded his hands on his knees. "So, Vic's gone?"

She made a face. "I thought I was ready to have this conversation with you, but when are you ever ready to admit your marriage has fallen apart?" She shrugged. "Yes. And despite what the boys want to think, I'm pretty sure he won't be coming back. Ever. Not to them, not to me."

Zach wanted to punch something. He couldn't, so he sat, ready to listen.

His sister had worked hard to become a nurse midwife. She'd studied night and day, working full-time, and should be able to relax a little now. As if working full-time delivering babies and mothering two kids wasn't already double-duty.

But she should be doing it with a loving husband by her side. Zach had been a groomsman at their wedding, eight years ago. He'd laughed and danced and toasted their future.

"What happened?" He kept his voice gentle, not wanting to make her cry, but the look on her face said that was probably inevitable. "Did he cheat on you, Jules?"

Her face held the answer he dreaded to see. "Oh, honey." He reached out and hugged her, letting her cry into his shoulder. "Have you been trying to be brave about this? How long has this been going on?"

"This time?"

Her reply hit Zach in the gut. "He's done this before?"

She nodded, snuffled and then blew her nose into the wad of tissues he handed her. "Yes. And I tried to be strong, taking my share of the blame..."

Zach's instant and protective reaction made her smile through her tears.

"Marriage isn't easy," she went on. "I knew that my grad school and clinical schedule wore on him."

"Wore on him?" Zach exclaimed. He ran a frustrated hand through his hair, not understanding. "What about on you? What kind of moron doesn't take care of the woman whose income helps pay the bills?"

"I thought it would be perfect," she confessed. The clutch of tissues in her hand showed wear, so he handed her a new bunch. "With Vic being a teacher, he'd be home early in the day to take care of the boys. And then he'd have weekends and summers off. Holiday vacations. It made perfect sense that once the boys were in school, our schedules would coexist to give the boys the best of both worlds. Working parents who could both spend time with them."

"What changed all that?"

"His current student teacher."

Now Zach really wanted to thrash Victor. "How old?"

"Twenty-two."

"Oh, Jules..."

She waved off his sympathy with a head shake. "I'm beyond the worst of it, Zach, really. Talking about it is hard, but I decided to make a clean break when he filed for divorce last month."

"And you waited all this time to tell us?"

"Because of me, I suppose." Marty's voice joined the conversation from the family-room level. He came up the stairs, crossed the room, pulled Julia out of the chair and gave her a big, long, paternal hug. His embrace instigated another round of tears.

Zach dragged his chair closer to Julia's. He did the same for the other side chair, giving his father a place to sit.

"Dad, I couldn't dump all this on you two when you'd just gone through the surgery. We were all worried about what we'd done to you, what your future would be. It was as if life piled so much on me at once, that when I got the official letter filing for divorce, I sent it off to Ethan, asked him to find me a good divorce attorney in the area and he did. The unfortunate side of this is that staying in Ithaca would keep the boys centered in the scandal because they'd be in the same school district. Since this was the second time he's cheated, I have no reason to believe he'll stop, whether he's married to me or someone else. So I figured I'd come here. See if there's a practice on this side of the state that could use a good, experienced midwife."

"You'll stay here, then?" Marty asked.

"I want to be where you are," Julia told him. "If you're both here, that's where I plan to be. I'm not foolish about how difficult it is to raise children on my own. And I'm not sure what kind of visitation Vic will want, if any, so a three-hour drive might not be the smartest thing to do, but keeping the boys in the middle of his drama isn't an option. Better that I make a move now, and get them grounded with family around. I don't want them to be the kids the other students talk about."

"You don't think Vic will want to see them?" Zach couldn't begin to wrap his brain around such an idea. "His own boys?"

"Judging from the little time he spent with them the past five years, my guess is no. But maybe I'm wrong." Julia met their combined gazes and shrugged, but her voice broke. "Maybe it was just me he didn't want to be around."

Marty said something not pretty under his breath and hugged her again.

Zach stood, angry at the foolishness of people. How stupid was his brother-in-law to not realize the gifts God had given him?

Piper's face swam before him, and an understanding deepened within him. Abandoned children bore all kinds of scars. Those you see, and those well-hidden.

But scars could fade, with time. And new skin would replace the old, given a chance to grow free and healthy.

Martin and Connor would be given that chance. And so would Piper, if Zach had anything to say about it.

CHAPTER NINE

PIPER PULLED THE PICKUP INTO the Kirkwood Lake Town Hall parking lot the next morning. She'd left Marty and Berto setting up scaffolding along the northern side of the big barn once milking was done. She'd taken the quick drive to Clearwater to pick up parts for the old John Deere. Now she needed to drop off sample flyers for the bicentennial committee to review.

She crossed the carpeted foyer of the recently renovated town building and paused at the clerk's desk. "Betty, can you tuck these into the bicentennial committee's mailbox for me, please?"

"Are these the historic flyers?" The town clerk approached the desk and reached out a hand, then crowed, delighted. "Piper, I love them."

"Good." Betty's approval made Piper smile. "I incorporated ideas from various factions. The original farms, the mills, the boarding house, the train trestle...all the things that have evolved into the current Kirkwood Lake."

"And the two one-room schoolhouses." Betty's expression said her appreciation went deep. "My mother's mother taught at this one." She pointed to a small clapboard building Piper had nestled in an upper corner of the flyer. "And my great-grandmother on my father's side was the high school principal of this one once they built a separate elementary school."

"So you like it."

"I love it," she declared. "And I'm sure the committee will too. We're so grateful you were willing to put these together. I know it probably seems like a lot of planning for an anniversary year..."

"It's not often a town celebrates two hundred years of being a town," Piper corrected her. "I think it's a wonderful idea and I know you've put a lot of effort in on this. That's what makes it fun, though. The whole town, working together. Seeing our past helps us plan for the future."

"Piper?"

A smooth voice called her name, too smooth. Too polished.

Piper turned and didn't pretend to smile at the current town supervisor. "Ron. What can I do for you?"

"May I see you a moment?"

She wanted to say no. Ron Palmeteer favored change in Kirkwood Lake. The fact that he got elected meant he had enough people on his side to make waves for the regular folks of Kirkwood, the ones who had lived in and worked in and molded this town for centuries. Ron talked big and acted small, two qualities Piper abhorred. But better she talk to him now than allow him to blindside her and the other local farmers. Ron and his upscale family weren't exactly farm-friendly.

She followed him into his office. He wore a patronizing smile, and that was almost enough to make her walk out, but she didn't. "What's up?"

"Vince and Linda have a firm offer on their farm."

She assumed that would happen soon, because their property was beautiful and well-maintained. Therefore this wasn't news. "To be expected."

"Of course." He waved a hand as if they were

simpatico. They weren't. "And you know that Wickshire Development is vying for waterway rights on the upper west shore."

"Yes." There were no waterway rights available. And that fact had kept Wickshire from creating a planned community with lakeshore access. McKinney Farm was the only parcel on that side of the lake with significant frontage, and McKinney Farm wasn't for sale.

"Which brings us to you." He withdrew a rolled-up map of the lake, unrolled it across his desk, and weighted the corners. "Here's Vince and Linda's land."

"Ron, I know where Vince and Linda live. We're neighbors. And friends. We've worked our farms together for years."

"Of course." His thin smile said he didn't think much of that. "And here's your land. Well," He cleared his throat to make a point and tapped a finger to the sprawl of McKinney Farm. "Yours and your brothers. And Mrs. McKinney, of course."

"And my sister Rainey."

He shrugged that off as inconsequential, as if Rainey meant nothing, and that put a burr between Piper's shoulder blades. Ron's brother Bob had been in and out of rehab for over a decade. Bob's youngest son had multiple DWIs and could no longer drive himself anywhere. Who was he to judge Rainey's past?

"I understand your family has been at odds about selling, even though this is by far the most lucrative time in our lives to be wheeling and dealing. Kirkwood Lake has enjoyed a resurgence, a situation that knows no bounds as long as we don't let sentimentality get in the way."

"Sentimentality?" Piper raised a brow, inviting him to continue, fairly sure he'd get to the point soon. And she was just as sure the point wouldn't be in her favor. "I suppose you could say that running a successful family farm has sentiment attached. But then, you've never been part of a family business, have you, Ron?"

"Corporate America grabbed me first." His smile widened.

Piper fought the urge to gag.

"In any case, we're at a crossroads here. A moment in time when large-scale thinking needs to overlook the narrow-mindedness of the past and embrace the vision of the future."

"In other words, you want things your way because your way is better." Piper had heard this all before, just not so blatantly. Which meant Ron had something up his sleeve.

"The town of Kirkwood Lake is serving you notice that we intend to access your lakefront property at fair market value to allow the building of sewer lines and recreational boating access for the good of the town as a whole."

He was trying to stake a claim of eminent domain on McKinney Farm. Not the whole thing, just the parts that made it prime developmental land, the lakeshore, reputedly worth well over a million dollars.

"You're trying to seize my property."

"No." Ron shook his head as if he were sincerely trying to do what was best for the town. The fact that he owned a thirty-seven acre parcel adjacent to Vince and Linda's land wasn't lost on Piper. If their land abutted the new sewer line, the value of his property skyrocketed. "I'm doing what I was elected to do, and that is to offer my business expertise to Kirkwood Lake to encourage growth and steady improvement."

"And once again McKinney Farm stands in your way." Piper drew herself more upright. "You understand I'll fight you on this, right? And that a good share of the town will join the fight? And you're up for reelection in two years. How do you think this will stand in your campaign?"

"Open your eyes, Piper." He waved to the window at his left. "Kirkwood Lake is changing."

"And not for the better. Inflated land values mean higher property taxes. How will people on a fixed income manage that?"

"Times change. People change. And old folks move on every day. Young people move in, educated people. Progressives."

She saw his aim clearly then, and it made her sick to her stomach. "You want a town filled with miniature versions of you. Well, it won't happen, Ron. Not on my watch. And if you think for a minute the town won't rise up against you on this, think again. You've pushed and people have backed down, a little at a time. But this." She jabbed an angry finger at his town map. "This isn't democracy. It's your quest for total world domination. It won't work."

He shrugged his shoulders as if she were nothing more than a pesky fly. "It will. Because your house is divided already. Read your history lessons, Piper. Lincoln said it best: A house divided cannot stand."

He was wrong. It would stand, and regardless of his goal to take her down, she'd make sure McKinney Farm survived.

She stormed out, climbed into the cab of her truck, turned on the engine and drove off before she let the angry tears come, because no way was she about to give Ron Palmeteer the satisfaction of seeing her cry.

"We should power-wash this first."

Berto scowled at the scaffolding, shrugged and nodded. "That would have been smart to do before we built the scaffold."

"I'll get mine and bring it over." Zach climbed off the tiered tubing, crossed the field, grabbed a bag full of cookies that Julia had baked early in the day and wheeled the heavy-duty sprayer back across the field.

"You could have put it in your SUV."

"Should have." Zach rubbed his upper arm to ease the knot he'd gotten by half pulling, half carrying the power washer through the hard sod. "That field is not exactly wheel-friendly."

He ran a barn hose to the sprayer, primed the engine, then stood back as his father blasted old, faded, flaking paint from the north side of the sprawling building.

Another engine pulled his attention. Piper drove the pickup truck into the yard, curved around the end of the barn, and stopped.

She didn't get out.

Piper McKinney rarely stopped moving. And she never parked and sat. Zach jogged across the front of the barns and pulled up short at the driver's door.

Her tears stopped him cold in his tracks.

The moment he realized she was crying, he had the urge to pummel all the bad guys on the planet to make things right for her again. Instead he opened the door, reached in and touched her shoulder. "Tell me who made you cry. I'll take care of it for you, honey."

Her lower lip quivered more. She'd taken off to run a few errands in town ninety minutes before. What could have happened in an hour and a half?

"The town is threatening to seize parts of the farm."

"They're what?" He couldn't wrap his brain around her words. "How do you know this?"

She climbed out of the cab, red-eyed and splotchy-looking, so the tears had been going on for a while. He pulled her in for a hug, letting her wet his shirtfront and sleeves with her tears. And when she took a couple of deep, long breaths, he stepped back and bent lower. "No one is going to take your farm. Not without going through me first. I barely like farms, but I'm willing to die for your right to run one."

A hinted smile said she appreciated his sentiment, but the smile deepened when he added, "Of course my lawyer brother will help, too. Free of charge."

"You think he will?"

Zach nodded. "Ethan's always on the side of the underdog. He'll eat this up. If it even gets that far. So tell me." He tipped her chin up and met her gaze, needing the facts. "What happened?"

"The town supervisor intends to use eminent domain along the northern road frontage of the farm to develop a sewer line for proposed development."

Zach understood the financial link between direct sewer lines and development. This was a huge and expensive step for the town to take, but he also knew the south end of the lakeshore was more friendly to increased development.

"And they want to confiscate the lakefront property for the good of the community and use it for a public boat launch and docking area, while paying us whatever their fair appraisal comes out to be."

"In a pig's eye." He released her shoulders, strode away, then walked back, arms braced, legs apart. "Who told you this?"

"Ron Palmeteer."

Zach ran a hand through his hair, then withdrew his cell phone. "Did he say when they were going to formally inform you of their intent?"

A sheriff's car rolled up the drive. Luke Campbell was driving. A young female deputy followed in a second car. While Piper and Zach waited, Luke Campbell cut the engine and swung out of the car. The young woman followed. Luke held an envelope in his hand, but his face said he detested the job he'd been given. "Piper, I've been ordered to give this to you."

She took the envelope from his hand, but didn't look up.

"Don't hate the messenger," Luke continued. "I'm not supposed to know what's in this," he nodded toward the vellum envelope she held, "but it's all anyone is talking about at the town hall. Folks are mad, Piper. We won't let them get away with this."

Tears reformed in Piper's eyes, and Zach read the sorrow there. After all her hard work, to have some aging guy in a bad suit try to jerk the rug out from under her...

It was wrong. No matter how he personally felt about farming, a person had the right to create and maintain a business on their own land within the parameters of the law. Piper, Lucia and Berto had done that. And more. They'd not only clung to the family farm, they'd improved it, and if the town supervisor and his board didn't understand the importance of that, he'd be glad to set them straight at the next town meeting.

"It's all right, Luke." Piper dashed away the tears with the heels of her hands. It made Zach want to protect her from bad days, crop failures, town supervisors and more. So much more.

"It's not all right." Luke reached out and gave her a hug, and when it lasted a little too long for Zach's liking, he cleared his throat. Loudly.

Luke backed off and grinned at Zach. "Understood." He turned Piper's way. "There's a town board meeting next Thursday night. We all plan to be there. And don't trust Palmeteer not to try to do something to force your hand or landlock your options. He stands to gain a whole lot of property value if Vince and Linda's land sells to a developer with sewer rights available. We can't let that happen."

"What if we're wrong, Luke?" Piper pulled a deep

breath and waved her right hand toward the farm surrounding them. "What if this is just a silly pipe dream like my brothers have been saying for years? What if it's time to take the money and run? Let the change come? What if I'm just being stubborn and unwilling to see the big picture?"

"Piper, *this* is the big picture." Zach put his hands on her shoulders and turned her toward the fields, the barns. "Don't allow narrow-minded people to make you second-guess yourself. 'Those who believe something can't be done should get out of the way of the people doing it.'"

"I love that quote." She smiled up at him and his heart took another step toward total, unequivocal involvement.

"Because you live that quote." He gave her shoulders a gentle squeeze and turned back to Luke. "Can you let the guys on your force know what's going down?"

"Will do. And with the number of DWIs Palmeteer's nephew has wiggled out of, he's got no friends in the sheriff's department. We all know the kid's a deadly accident waiting to happen and that Ron and Bob just keep buying his way out of the system."

"Agreed. I'll pass the word at the barracks tomorrow and we need a letter to the local paper. You." Zach aimed his gaze to Piper. "Are you ready to put your heart on the page and start a revolution?"

She nodded. "As long as someone checks my spelling."

"Good thing Julia's here." Zach smiled and brushed a fingertip against her nose. "She's my go-to person for spelling advice."

Someone shut the power washer off. The sudden silence made Piper, Zach and Luke stand still, looking at one another. Piper took the first breath and broke the silence. "Do you think we can stop this? Really?"

"Not think. Know." Luke grinned, tipped his cap and went back to his car. He gave a high sign to the other deputy and they rolled around the circular drive, back toward the road.

Piper scowled, kicked the dirt and worked her jaw. "You know the worst thing?"

"No. What?" Zach stood quiet and still, wondering just how much support they would get overall. That concerned him because he knew opinions varied from one end of the lake to the other.

"Not one of us raised a fuss when Palmeteer and his buddies started changing little things like adjusting zoning codes so you couldn't have a mother-in-law apartment without the town's permission. Why should you need permission for families to share the same house? That's ridiculous, but we were all too busy making a living to launch a counterattack. Or when they redrew agricultural lines near the southern shore that pushed farms farther away from the town center. Right now I feel like I came into an ongoing game of chess and it's my move, only I have no idea where my king and queen are hiding. That means they're already in jeopardy."

Zach didn't agree. "You might be late to the game but you've got tradition and farm management on your side. I can't believe the Department of Agriculture and Markets will think this is a good idea. If one town bullies a farm, it sets precedent for other towns to do the same. Ag and Markets won't let that happen."

"You think we're in trouble."

He looped an arm around her shoulders and headed them both toward the house. "I think we've *got* trouble, but we can win. We'll fight. We'll win. But it will probably get ugly."

"What will get ugly?" Marty noted Zach's arm around Piper's shoulders, smiled, then frowned. "What's wrong? Are you crying? Did you make her cry? What's the matter with you?"

"I did nothing of the sort. She cried all by herself. With a little help from the stupid town."

"He didn't make me cry, Marty." Piper half laughed, trying to deflect the opposing glares of father and son. "No, it's this." She held the envelope aloft. "The town is trying to seize parts of the farm by using eminent domain."

Marty said something under his breath that made Zach's eyebrows shoot up. He paced toward the barn, then back their way. "What are they saying?"

"That with Vince and Linda's land going on the market, once it's sold they want to have an easement of my land for a sewer district to be established from the lakeshore to the western boundary of Vince and Linda's land."

"Subdivisions. Housing. All overlooking that pretty piece of lake we see right there." Marty turned and pointed down the hill. The McKinneys' beautiful corner of Kirkwood Lake waterfront sat still and pristine there, dotted with deciduous trees and a few evergreens around the wooden gazebo. Pastoral and sweet, the land sat at water's edge, a refuge and respite from the busyness of life.

"They intend to seize the lakefront to use for public and private boating launches and docks."

"They what?" Marty turned quickly. He stared at the lake, then at Piper and Zach. "They want to seize the lakefront too?"

"It's the only remaining open ground on the northwest shore." Piper stared at the property in question, then shifted her attention back to Zach and Marty. "My great-great-grandparents settled this land. They carved this farm out of the forest. They worked night and day, then bought other parcels here and there. McKinney Farm grew and did well until…" She heaved a breath, bit her lip, then shrugged. "Until my mother left us and took two-hundred and fifty-thousand dollars as alimony from my father."

"Ouch." Marty's expression showed shock and disbelief at that figure.

"Piper." Zach had no trouble reading the reality of her mother's abandonment in Piper's face. He tugged her closer and held her, not caring that his father watched, just knowing he wanted to help. Some way. Somehow.

Piper shrugged out of his grip, face grim. "I've got a letter to write."

"And I have a barn to paint soon as it's dry," Marty announced. "That power sprayer is a wonderful piece of equipment, son. It would have taken me days to scrape that barn wall properly." Marty headed toward Zach's house. "I'm grabbing coffee, then running an errand. By the time I get back I should be ready to paint."

Zach raised his cell phone. "And I'm calling Ethan for his advice. And getting back to the deck."

Marty met Zach's gaze. "If you'd rather I help you on the deck, I can do that. The barn's been there a while. It'll still need painting in a week. I know you're behind."

He was, but right now he needed to take a breath, call his brother, examine Piper's options, then build a deck. The deck wasn't going anywhere, although he hated seeing a job half-done.

"I'm good, Dad, but thanks. No reason I can't keep building once I'm back at work."

He punched in his brother's number on his cell phone, then paced while he waited for Ethan to pick up. While he walked back and forth, he scanned the farm surrounding him, seeing it with greater clarity now.

The family farm had fallen on tough times when a marriage fell apart. No wonder Piper clung hard and long to a family legacy that had almost caved before. She wasn't just staking a claim on a farm, but on the family that had developed it. Worked it, generation after generation.

He watched her dash up the back steps of the plain white farmhouse and knew she was determined to thwart the town's efforts. No matter what the town offered financially, losing the lakefront access diminished the farm's value exponentially and changed the northwest shore forever. And if it had that kind of financial effect now, how much more would that pretty piece of shoreline be worth in ten years? Twenty?

One way or another he'd help Piper keep hold of what was hers. He couldn't go back and undo the sale of his father's farm. He'd bear that on his shoulders until the day he passed from the earth.

But Piper's dream was here. And no group of political cronies would be allowed to wrench it from her.

CHAPTER TEN

"YOU DON'T LOOK READY." ZACH'S dubious voice held a strong note of misgiving.

Ready?

Piper turned from the computer, saw how clean and dressed up Zach was, and wanted to kick herself. They were supposed to go on a date tonight, but after this morning's political bombshell, she'd assumed—wrongly, it seemed—that they'd be sitting home, pouting.

"Fifteen minutes." He stepped through the door and tapped his watch. "We've got reservations and luckily I assumed you were running late when I saw you stomping in from the milking parlor twenty minutes ago."

"Fifteen minutes? No way can I—"

"Fourteen. Clock's ticking, Piper."

He wasn't taking no for an answer, and that made her feel good inside. Treasured.

She hurried upstairs, took the fastest shower ever, slipped into the second dress she owned since Zach had already seen the first one, and added an ankle bracelet to her left foot, earrings to her ears and a touch of mascara. She slid her feet into sling-back high heels, wondered if sandals might be better, decided against it because her toes looked horrible and was back downstairs in the allotted time.

Zach whistled. "Impressive."

"The timing or the girl?"

"Both. But mostly the girl."

His eyes added certainty to the words, and that made a flush rise up from somewhere deep within her. When Zach offered a compliment, the weight of sincerity made it special.

She'd never experienced that before and decided she loved it. Honesty, appreciation and a sense of humor, rolled into one great cop, heart and soul.

A keeper.

Was he?

He offered her his arm in a most courtly fashion.

She accepted it and proceeded down the back steps with him.

"Trooper Zach and Piper, sitting in a tree! K-i-s-s-i-n-g," a neighbor girl spelled out from a table near the ice cream window. "First comes love. Then comes marriage. Then comes a baby in a baby carriage!"

"Junie!"

Zach opened the door to his SUV for Piper and waved to the mother. "Nothing I haven't been thinking myself, ma'am."

"Do tell." The young mother saw Piper's look and laughed out loud. "Trooper, I do believe you've struck Piper speechless and that's a rarity around here."

"Almost as good as sighting an evening grosbeak before the leaves have fallen."

"You're a bird-watcher?" Piper leaned out the open window of the SUV.

Zach tipped his head to Junie's mother, grinned and climbed into the driver's seat. "I prefer the term 'birder,' but yes. I am. Check the glove box."

Piper hit the latch. The glove box held several books about birds, with detailed pictures and descriptions. "Whoa. You are a birder. For real."

He steered the SUV down the drive and onto the road, then tapped the console box between them. "Equipment."

She sent him a funny look, then opened the box. Two pairs of binoculars sat inside, clearly well-used. "When do you do this?"

"When I need time to think. To pray. To figure things out."

"Do you hate my barn cats?" she wondered out loud. "Because their primary job is to catch rodents. Rats, mice, moles and the occasional dead snake don't bother me at all, but they do catch birds now and again. Is that a deal-breaker?"

He laughed and shook his head. "Not if they keep the field mice and baby rats away from my house, too. And did you know you have a nest of kittens in the far barn?"

"No." She turned his way, eager. "Moonbeam had her babies?"

"If Moonbeam is the orange cat with dark orange stripes—"

"No, that's Pumpkin. Moonbeam is lighter and has a white belly."

"Then Pumpkin has babies. Four of them. Three dark, one light."

"I love baby animals. And no matter how often I see a calf being born, I still love the experience. When all goes well, of course. Your father said he's the same way."

"He is," Zach admitted. Funny, he hadn't thought about it in those terms, that his father treasured the miracle of birth. He'd only looked at the financial side of things, that his father worked night and day to build a bigger, better business, when the reality was maybe the older man simply loved what he was doing.

And if that was the case, why didn't Zach see it sooner?

Because he was just as stubborn and doggedly determined as his father.

"Do you have favorite birds?"

Zach mulled her question, then nodded. "Tiny ones."

"Really?" His admission seemed to delight her. "You like little birds?"

"They're amazing." He turned toward Clearwater and waved to an older couple out for an evening stroll along Lake Road. "They defy the odds consistently. Their size. Their strength. Their versatility. You thought I'd like raptors, didn't you?"

Piper couldn't deny it. "They're big. Strong. They soar and dive and float and show off all their prowess. Yeah, I'd have taken you for a big bird kind of guy. And we have two bald eagle nesting sites not far from here as they stage a comeback. And they are crazy majestic."

"Sure are." Zach acknowledged that with a nod, then went on. "I'm a finch man. And nuthatches. And buntings, orioles. I'm installing feeders to draw more to your back field. That way I can see them from my patio, but it keeps the squirrels from deciding my house would make a great winter quarters."

"There's some kind of cute little bird that lives in that big stand of spruce trees at the back property line," Piper told him. "They're brownish-gold and they sing like crazy."

"Cute little bird." Zach nodded thoughtfully. "Now there's a scientific description for you."

She laughed and batted his arm. "Check them out yourself, bird-man."

"Better yet, you and I can take a walk out there and see what we find together." Zach posed the question at a stoplight and turned, watching for her reaction. "Look at the birds," he quoted softly from Christ's Sermon on the Mount. "They do not sow or reap..."

"And yet our Heavenly Father feeds them." She faced him more fully, nodding. "I'd like that, Zach." She half whispered the answer, reading the question in his eyes, the tilt of his head. "I'd like to go walking with you."

Her words tugged his heart wider.

He'd been given a new glimpse into Piper McKinney today. A whole new perspective on her workaholic nature. If you needed to keep a family legacy alive, with few people to help, you did what needed to be done. That was Piper.

She didn't *want* to work night and day. She just wanted to keep a piece of her historic family intact, a unit that broke irrevocably when her mother left years ago. It wasn't so much the farm as it was the *family* farm. That was a concept he now understood fully.

Zach had two loving parents for decades, and he'd still whined about his father's choice of profession.

Piper had only one parent for over half of her life, and lost him several years ago, but did she complain?

No.

She hunkered down and did what needed to be done, despite the odds against her. And looked mighty good doing it.

"What are you thinking?" She reached a hand to his arm as they pulled into the parking lot of a long-established steak house. "You got quiet."

"You know what I was thinking?" He turned her way, cupped her cheek and leaned in to kiss her lips. "I was contemplating what an amazing woman you are."

She pulled back instantly, surprised and uncomfortable with the compliment, which only made Zach more determined to accustom her to hearing sweet things. Loving things.

He ignored her reaction and smiled at her, holding her gaze with his eyes and her cheek in one hand. "You work hard and rarely complain."

Her eye roll said she might protest more than he thought, and just hadn't done it around him.

He smiled wider. "You're not afraid to tackle big jobs

and little jobs. You've taught those precious girls to be sweet, nice and respectful most of the time."

"With Lucia's help. And mostly following her lead."

"You're dogged, focused, smart—"

She winced a little when he said smart, the same reaction he'd gotten earlier when he asked about writing the letter. Did she think she wasn't smart because spelling gave her trouble?

She was running a quarter-million-dollar farm and doubted herself because she couldn't spell? Ridiculous.

But the look in her eye said it might be more true than not, so he'd tackle that insecurity later. Right now, a kiss was in order. Soft. Gentle. And when he managed to leave her speechless for the second time in less than thirty minutes, Zach Harrison climbed out of the SUV, pleased with himself.

"Flowers." Piper stared at the floral basket in the center of their dinner table and sighed, enchanted. "Zach, they're gorgeous."

"For you." He tipped his gaze to the basket and nudged her forward. "There's a card."

His smile said he liked surprising her, and Piper discovered she enjoyed the feeling as well. Gentle words, sweet praise, long looks from those gorgeous blue eyes...

Her heart stuttered, then calmed as she read the card. "Thank you for our first date. I'm already hoping for many more to come."

She turned and looked up at him, but she did it slowly. Thoughtfully. He might think he knew a lot about her, but it was easy in the glow of attraction to brush aside deeper issues. And the McKinney family came with plenty of those. "I come with baggage, Zach."

He tweaked her nose and held out her chair. "Don't we all?"

"Mine are living, breathing people. A family full of people who depend on me. Depend on the farm's success. And the dairy store."

"Why should that make a difference?" Zach wondered. He accepted menus from the waiter, gave their drink order, then switched his attention back to Piper.

"Because most girls come with just themselves." She leaned closer, determined to be frank. "Berto and Lucia have nothing except their investment of time in that farm. The girls will need care until they're grown. And you're not real big on farming, so I don't see how an attraction…"

He caught her left hand, lifted it for a kiss, and smiled at her. Just her. A full, magnum-force smile that said more than words ever could.

"Well, I can't possibly warn you off when you look at me like that." She sighed, dramatic, then smiled. "But you know what I mean."

He held her hand lightly, waited while the waiter came back with their drinks, placed an appetizer order and then met her gaze. "Wanna talk baggage?"

Put that way, she suddenly wasn't all that sure, but she nodded. "Yes."

"I sold my father's farm out from under him."

Maybe because that was the last thing she expected to hear, it hurt the most. She'd read the longing in Marty's eye, sadness bowing his shoulders. The ease with which he handled the cows, equipment and routine. Marty Harrison was obviously a man well-schooled with farm technology and animal husbandry. "Why would you do that?"

Zach made a face, but the expression did nothing to mask the pain in his eyes. "He got sick. Very sick. It wasn't long after my mother died in a car accident. He started losing function, physical and mental."

"Oh, Zach." Piper cringed and squeezed his hand. "That had to be so hard because none of you were close by. Right?"

"Right. He started forgetting things. Getting lost. One day he'd be fine, the next day he'd forget my name. And it kept going on like that, until we didn't dare leave him alone at the farm. He'd fall as if he was tripping over things but there was nothing in his way. And then the medical center told us he had early-onset Alzheimer's. That's why it hit so fast and hard, because the early-onset variety takes hold quickly."

"But he's fine." Piper didn't know a lot about Alzheimer's, but she knew there was no cure. So how could Marty be doing so well now?

Shadows darkened Zach's gaze as he met her look of question. "Because they were wrong, Piper. When things got so bad that Dad was a danger to himself and others, we found a nice nursing home for him. Ethan lives downstate, Julia was pregnant and crazy busy with her midwife practice and Martin, so I was appointed power of attorney to take care of things. We had to liquidate everything to pay for Dad's care once his insurance ran out."

"So you had to sell the farm." She leaned closer, held tight, and let her fingers warm his. "It's not like you had a choice, Zach."

"I did, though." He studied her hand. A tiny muscle clenched in his left cheek. He breathed deep and gave a slight shrug. "I could have taken a leave and run the farm. We had plenty of help. And like yours, our farm was a family enterprise. Dad was the third generation. I could have been the fourth, at least long enough to see how things would go."

"But you had no reason to believe he'd get better, right?" She paused, puzzled, then asked, "How did he get better? Because there's no cure for Alzheimer's."

"The doctors here discovered the error and rediagnosed him."

"Oh, Zach." Concern and empathy flowed through her. She could envision the whole scenario, the grief and sadness surrounding a grim diagnosis and prognosis, the hard decisions that had to be made…

And then to find out it was all a mistake?

Piper couldn't imagine the stress that put on Zach's heart. His soul. Men like him took a great deal on themselves. She could see he'd internalized the guilt of being the decision-maker. "I'm so sorry this all happened."

"Me, too." He squeezed her hand and frowned. "Two months ago we got Dad an opening in Kirkhaven, the long-term care facility near Clearwater. We'd been on the waiting list there, it was so much closer to me and I knew it was a good adult care facility. I was ready to close on my house, Dad would be moving closer. Everything seemed ideal. We no sooner got him there than the doctor called me and said he thought Dad was misdiagnosed. That he had something that looks like Alzheimer's, but was correctable. He called it 'normal pressure hydrocephalus' and said a fairly simple operation to shunt excess fluid away from Dad's brain would clear things up."

"I'd have been over-the-top angry at the first medical center," Piper said. That misdiagnosis had robbed Marty of more than time. It had taken a family legacy and ruined a relationship between a father and son.

So this is why Zach looked so guilt-ridden around his father. Why he watched him quietly when he thought no one was looking. "So what's the prognosis now?"

"He's going to be fine," Zach told her. The appetizers arrived, and he waited until the waiter had left again before continuing. "And we're all grateful for that, but we feel so guilty for making decisions that took his whole life from him. And then to find out we were wrong just makes a bad situation worse."

"Can he start again?"

Zach shrugged. "I brought it up once and he just about bit my head off."

"He needs time."

Zach nodded. "And being stubborn, he won't go for therapy."

Piper looked at him, surprised. "What's therapy going to do besides cost him more time and money?"

"Therapy can be life-saving."

"It can, but in his case, Marty just needs to be busy. Handling cattle and tractors and big machines that make him feel like he's in charge."

"Farm therapy."

"Exactly!" Piper smiled. "He's getting that for free at my place. You can see how much more relaxed he is by hanging out at the farm. Helping. Working. Getting things in some semblance of order."

"Yes."

"Zach." She ignored the savory-smelling clams casino and the chilled plate of shrimp, and laid her hand against his face, his cheek. "Your mistake was due to someone else's error. Not yours. But your dad's recovery, regardless of the farm sale, is the stuff dreams are made of. He's got a second chance to do whatever he wants to do. And so do you."

"Me?" He straightened a little, perplexed.

"To fix things between you. To mend old fences. Right old wrongs. A second chance, Zach." She smiled right at him and hoped he read what she couldn't exactly say, that second chances were a wonderful thing and not everyone gets that opportunity. "Grab it. Run with it. Take full advantage of a God-given gift to make things right."

Her words softened his face. Brightened his eyes. "Can we eat first?"

She laughed. "Yes, because I starved myself all day

worrying. But, now. Here. With you?" She hoped her sincerity lightened the gravity of the moment. "I'm ready to grab hold of the next chapter in my life. Whatever it might be."

He smiled, then slid the wooden trivet holding the plate of hot, seasoned clams her way. "I believe it starts with these. But first." He raised his glass of lemon tea and tipped his gaze to hers. "A toast."

Piper smiled, raised her glass and waited.

"To new beginnings."

Her heart sang. But her conscience pinched. A fresh start. It was a lovely concept. But he had no clue what he was getting into. Nevertheless, she touched her glass to his and smiled. "Here. And now."

His look deepened as he grabbed a shrimp. "Okay, you've heard my story. Now, what about yours?"

She savored a clam, decided that clams and bacon should always be served together, and said, "You got the gist of it today. The farm's been shortchanged emotionally and financially since my mother took off eighteen years ago."

"Does she have any contact with you?"

"None." Piper wasn't sure she'd want to see her mother if she *did* initiate contact after all this time. How sad was that?

"With your brothers?"

"Not that I know of." Piper sipped her water, frowning slightly. "She wanted a new life, free from the constraints of the farm. And her family."

"I'm sorry." Zach's face said he couldn't imagine that pain, but Piper had realized something as she matured. Her mother had left the family emotionally years before leaving physically with her boyfriend. That had made understanding the separation easier.

Accepting it? Another matter entirely.

"The plus side is I inherited Lucia and Berto. I love them." She had no problem admitting this to Zach.

"Lucia's not like having my own mother. More like an older best friend. I can talk frankly with her, we can make farm plans together, we work well together and she loves me the way I am."

"I kind of like you the way you are too."

She laughed at the puppy-dog expression on his face. "Well, thank you."

"And now tell me about Reilich."

She'd sensed the question was coming, and she thought she'd prepared herself, but every time someone mentioned Hunter's name the term "epic fail" swam before her eyes. She hauled in a breath, looked anywhere but at Zach, then hiked a shoulder. "I was young and stupid. Thank God there are no laws against that, or I'd be doing time right now."

"I don't know him." Zach watched her as he spoke, studying her reaction. He didn't want to ruin the night with old war stories, but he wanted her to feel comfortable around him. Able to share anything. "I came to Troop A before he was put in jail, but I was stationed in Fillmore, and his crimes were centered in the Clearwater area."

"How did you know about him?"

He didn't hesitate. "Luke told me."

"Snitch."

He smiled. "He knew I was interested when I offered to punch him for smiling at you and he wished me luck. Or something like that."

"Luke's a good guy."

"He is. And he's had a bunch of rough breaks, but when he told me about Reilich, I realized why the uniform might be a deal-breaker for you. And yet..." He leaned forward and grazed her chin with his right hand. "I was hoping you'd see beyond the uniform eventually."

"Oh, I did." She smiled. "But I also saw an already

tenuous neighbor relationship going down the tubes if this attraction went bad, and farmers have enough hard times with neighbors these days. And you picked on my roosters."

"Which I'll never do again," he promised, laughing. "Although with Julia and the boys at my place, the roosters will be drowned out by the sound of two brothers wrestling. Puppies yipping. And country music playing in the background."

"That's not a bad scenario, Zach."

"It isn't, but don't change the subject. You were engaged to Reilich."

"I hate to admit it, but yes. And before you decide that I'm not the sharpest tool in the shed, let me assure you he was very good at what he did."

Bingo.

He'd hit the exposed nerve again, the intelligence issue. He leaned closer. "Piper, you're one of the smartest, most ambitious and innovative women I've *ever* met. Why don't you see that about yourself?"

"Having detectives second-guess your intelligence as they grill you multiple times about how you could have had a close, personal relationship with a man who engineered a racketeering payback scheme in the local towns leads one to question her judgment. And find it sadly lacking."

Zach could see how that played out. The detectives wanting to ferret out all the information they could, thinking Piper might have had a clue. Seen something. Been involved.

But Zach had met guys like Reilich before. They loved leading two lives. He was only sorry Piper got caught in the guy's schemes, but that was the past, and truth to tell, he had a few relationships that never should have gone beyond date number two, but did. "Let's level this playing field. Start fresh. I'm beginning to like farms a lot more than I ever thought possible."

Her heightened color said she read the meaning behind his words and his smile.

"And I think you're losing your aversion to cops as we speak." He grinned, picked up a shrimp and handed it to her. "While these are amazing, my budget thinks pan-fried fish fresh from the lake are some mighty good eats."

"Perch."

"And walleyes."

"You guys need to take the boat out." Piper finished the shrimp, sighed and refused his offer of another one. Today's drama had postponed Zach's outing with Julia and the boys. "The boys would love to go out on the water. I've got half a dozen kid-sized life preservers in the shed by the shore and four adult-sized."

"Can we take the girls sometime, too?"

"They'd love it, so yes." Piper smiled at him. "I know I work too much. I know I should do more things with them. And Lucia and Berto are both non-swimmers, so they wouldn't think of stepping foot in that boat, but I was brought up on the water. I can sail, row, troll, fish and I'm pretty good on horseback, so I'm carrying a trailer-load of guilt that I can't make time to offer the girls that same kind of experience."

"They're five. There's time yet. And now there are more grown-ups around." He hoped she'd realize that he intended, one way or another, to stay around. Hopefully as more than a neighbor.

"If Palmeteer has his way, I'll have plenty of time on my hands in two years."

"He won't, Piper." Zach leveled a direct look her way. "I've talked to Ethan—"

"And he says they don't have a leg to stand on, right? Please agree with that statement, wholeheartedly."

"Not exactly." Zach couldn't appease her dishonestly, but he actually liked what Ethan did say better. "He told me we should come out fighting early and strong. Get people fired up. He said it's much easier to stop or thwart an effort like this at the beginning than once it's gone to the court system. Politicians want to be reelected. If we can rally the town around us and protest this in a big way, Palmeteer'll be more likely to back down and throw the idea out."

"He doesn't like to back down," Piper warned him. "When he ran his home remodeling business, he loved taking over smaller companies, incorporating them into his own, and then letting people go. His big picture has only one viewpoint: his. And he's not afraid to hang folks out to dry."

"Which means you're concerned he'll air your personal family business to gain leverage."

"There's plenty of it to go around." Piper ticked off her fingers. "My mother took off with another man, the farm's in shaky financials, although improving annually, the boys hate the farm and would think nothing of undermining me and the supervisor knows that. I had an eighteen-month-long relationship with a man who is now a convicted felon, and my sister did time for holding up a convenience store at gunpoint when she was seventeen. If that's not bad enough, she then ran off and left twin toddlers six years later for no reason. If airing dirty laundry is on Palmeteer's to-do list, the McKinneys have given him ample ammunition."

The list sounded intimidating, even to Zach, and not much intimidated a state trooper. "We'll figure this out. I promise."

She smiled at him, and he read the joy in the smile, but he also recognized acceptance. Piper understood the cards were stacked against her. She'd fight, but she was willing to acknowledge that Palmeteer's methods might hurt a lot of people she cared about. And no way would she let that happen.

Neither would Zach, but as a cop, he'd been privy to a wealth of maneuvers in his eleven years on the force.

Palmeteer didn't stand a chance.

CHAPTER ELEVEN

"S O." CHAS LOOKED UP FROM the line of rapidly filling glass bottles of 2 percent milk. "You got served by the town yesterday, same as we did, right?"

There was no mistaking the note of triumph in his voice, and that meant he and Colin had already jumped on the supervisor's bandwagon. "If you mean did Ron Palmeteer and his cronies send me legal notice that they'd like to illegally seize part of our historic family farm, then yes, I did. But you and I would see that differently, Chas."

"Always have, always will," he agreed, then shrugged. "It's useless to go on resisting, Piper. You can chase rainbows on your own time and your own dime, but it's not fair to Colin and me to hang on to this place year after year."

Piper made note of the temperature readings on her computerized tablet. "I'll say. You take a generous paycheck and do almost nothing."

"I get things done," he retorted. "I'm just not manic like you. Obsessed. And I'd rather be doing anything else."

"Then do it."

Zach's voice interrupted their midday conversation. Piper turned, surprised.

So did Chas. The college gal working the cooler area stopped mid-step.

Piper recovered first. "Off to work?" Tension thrummed in the thin space separating the two men. Piper ignored the rise of emotions and centered herself between them purposely.

"Yes. I just wanted to stop by and say how much I enjoyed our evening together." He smiled at her with a kind, gentle gaze of affection, then addressed Chas directly. "I was raised on a farm. I hated it. But I didn't stay there and make everyone else's life miserable. I got an education, got a job and worked my way up. Staying here to annoy everyone around you isn't going to cut it forever. You might want to start thinking about that. Sooner rather than later."

Chas started forward, but Piper held up a restraining hand. "Zach—"

He silenced her with a look, stepped to her right, squared his shoulders and aimed a laser-beam look at her brother. "We respect women where I come from. We work hard. And we follow the Thumper rule. From where I stand, you're 0-for-3 and that's not putting me in good humor, McKinney."

"You're threatening me?"

Piper was tempted to jump in, but it actually felt good to have someone else take her side. Someone big, strong, smart and well-spoken.

Of course, his Glock carried its own special brand of backup.

"I'm actually making you a promise that from this point forward your sister will be protected from abuse, including emotional, physical and verbal. Got it? Chas?" Zach stretched out Chas's name as if challenging him, but Chas had the good sense to back down.

"Generally we occupy separate work areas, so your big bad cop act means nothing to me."

"Then we understand each other." Zach shifted his attention back down to Piper.

She met his look, half-ready to scold him for butting into family business, but his expression made her reassess.

In two sentences, he'd gotten Chas to be quiet. That could be a new record because Chas almost never stopped grumbling. If Piper had the cold, hard cash, she'd buy him out just to enjoy the silence.

She owed Zach thanks, but knew his methods could backfire. Getting Chas and Colin riled up would only put them more solidly in the supervisor's corner. But they were already on Palmeteer's side, so did it really matter? Maybe she'd been too careful in standing her ground. Of course having a big, stern, weapon-carrying cop on her side wasn't exactly a bad thing. She walked to the back door of the dairy room with him. "Have a good first night back."

He nodded and gripped her shoulders. "I will. But if you need me for anything while I'm gone," he raised his voice just enough for it to carry over the sound of the processing equipment, "call me. Okay?"

"I will."

He leaned down, planted a soft kiss to her temple and squeezed her hand. "See ya."

"Yes."

Chas snorted as Zach crossed the gravel drive to get to his SUV, but he stayed quiet for the rest of the afternoon. Four straight hours of no one harping at her, berating her or mocking her methods.

She owed Zach Harrison something special because it was the first half day of fairly decent behavior her brother had shown in years. And that felt nicer than she'd ever imagined.

She closed the doors later that afternoon, walked through the retail area to see how things were going, and grinned approval to Noreen and Jen behind the counter.

The store was busy, a wonderful thing, but Jen and her

sister Ada would be heading back to college in three weeks. Noreen would want to help full-time come fall, but there was no way the elderly woman could handle the rigor of those hours. Which meant they'd be shorthanded.

She stepped out the door and turned toward the house, ready for a shower and a tall iced coffee.

Rainey stood ten feet away, watching her.

Rainey.

Here.

Now.

Piper didn't know how to react. Her first instinct was to hug her sister, but reality nipped that in a heartbeat.

She'd left her babies. She'd left Lucia, Piper and Berto. She'd disappeared without a trace after they'd stood by her through her trial, conviction and incarceration.

And then she'd walked out on two perfectly beautiful, wonderful children without so much as a goodbye.

"What do you want?" Was that cold, hard tone her voice? Was this her, standing arms crossed, glaring at Rainey?

You bet it was, and Rainey could get herself back to wherever she'd been for three long, silent years and—

"Larraina?" Berto's joyous and welcoming voice overshadowed Piper's animosity. *"Aqui? Mi carino! Ven aqui, nina bonita!"*

Berto engulfed the tall, slim woman in his bearlike embrace, tears streaming, his voice muttering endearments mixed with thankful prayer.

Piper stood there, caught in time, gripped between warring emotions. Before her stood a beautiful woman who'd left without a backward glance. How could she forgive that?

But the joy in Berto's voice called out Piper's selfishness. And the girls...Dorrie and Sonya. The girls had their mother back. Hadn't Piper dreamed of that for years as a child? Wishing, praying, begging God to send her mother back?

He hadn't and she'd reconciled herself to that eventually.

But the twins were young. Sweet. Trusting. Surely they deserved a second chance at their mother's love.

"Larraina?"

Lucia's voice broke through Piper's internal battle. She turned toward the house and saw Lucia come down the steps. Disbelief colored Lucia's bland, brown face, but hesitation slowed her trek down the sidewalk.

"Mama."

"Lucia, see, she has returned and in good health, no?"

Berto's excitement begged Lucia to ignore the past, forget the years of silence and welcome the prodigal with open arms.

Lucia shushed him with a fierce look. "You have returned as quietly as you left, daughter."

Rainey met her mother's gaze and blinked once, slowly.

"You think to come back here after three years of silence and resume your place?"

Rainey stood her ground, letting Lucia speak her piece.

"You have worried me, you have worried Piper, you have tortured your sweet Uncle Humberto with your silence, and yet you believe you are welcome here, at this table, where your children have wondered for three long years where their mother has gone?"

"I have come to make amends." Rainey didn't back down, she didn't cower. Piper had to hand it to her: she'd grown up a lot in those three years, because Lucia was a formidable force when angry. And still Rainey didn't cringe or come undone.

Piper was pretty sure she would have under similar circumstances. She motioned to Lucia. "The twins?"

"Asleep."

"Good." Rainey faced her mother. "That will give us time to talk."

"So now you want to talk?" Lucia raised a hand of dismissal. "After all this time, you show up here and want to talk? Is it that you want to explain why you left here and had us worry so? Why you left your babies, *las niñas preciosas*? Why I no hear from you for three long years to find out if you breathe, if you be dead? Bah!"

Lucia turned her back on Rainey, a physical dismissal, but Rainey moved around the front of her mother and faced her. "All you have said is true, but there are things you don't know. Things that would have affected all of us." She redirected her gaze to Piper and settled it there. "Things that would have put this family in an even greater tailspin."

"You talk of something, but explain nothing!" Lucia glared, three years of temper rising, but Piper read something in Rainey's gaze that made her inhale slowly.

"Lucia. We should take this inside. Please."

Lucia stopped, surprised, and glanced around. A couple of customers had driven in, unnoticed until this moment.

Chagrin darkened the older woman's face. Empathy for her welled within Piper. Lucia had gone the distance for all of them, repeatedly, and had so little to show for it. The boys dismissed her completely. Rainey abandoned her. And Berto appeared upset that she was angry at Rainey's sudden return, as if the previous three years could be swept away, chaff on the wind.

Lucia marched across the drive, up the walk and into the house.

"Come." Berto looped an arm around his niece's shoulders, protective and kind, and his warmth shamed Piper. "You come in, you eat, you skin-and-bones girl. But you so beautiful, *mi* Larraina. I miss you so much!"

Piper followed behind, unsure what to say.

Hadn't she just dealt with half-a-day's worth of Chas's attitude? And now the prodigal returns just when Piper felt like she was starting a new chapter in her life?

And how to explain the convicted felon adopted sister to law-abiding state trooper Zach?

She swallowed a growl that threatened to overtake her from within. Right now she'd like to do something very physical for long hours, working out the anger and frustration grabbing her from within, but the adult Piper couldn't go pitch hay at the moment.

She had to listen. Hear things out. Pay attention, open-minded. That seemed like the very last thing she wanted to do.

Zach drove home, yawning. Two weeks of a daytime schedule put his sleep habits at odds with this evening shift. Three hours of overtime had added to his sleep deprivation. He headed north on Lake Road, made the left onto Watkins Ridge, then noticed lights at Piper's house.

There were never lights on at this hour. Not in the two months he'd been living around the corner from her. Early morning, yes, when she and Berto got up for milking, but now, when it was an hour past midnight?

That never happened.

Should he check things out? What if she was sick? Or the girls? What if—?

The light blinked out as he considered his options, leaving the house in darkness, but Zach couldn't dismiss the uneasiness welling within him.

If Piper was hurting, he wanted to help. He'd never felt such a draw to anyone before. He'd dated a lot of women over the years. He'd had a couple of long-term relationships before he moved to Troop A's area, but none of them compelled him to action like these few weeks spent with Piper McKinney.

Was that ridiculous? Was he asking for trouble, dating

someone whose family held no small amount of animosity toward police? And a farmer, besides?

He drove on, hesitant, wishing he had the right to go to her door and check on her, but pretty sure they'd think he was crazy. And he was crazy, he realized as he pulled the SUV into the garage next to his sister's minivan. Crazy about Piper. The kids and the goat made the whole package that much sweeter.

Check it out or you'll never sleep tonight.

He growled, parked the SUV, climbed out and was greeted by the anxious bellow of a cow in the McKinneys' far pasture. The bellow sounded once more, loud and long. This wasn't an impatient cow, waiting to be milked and tired of standing.

This was a cow in trouble, laboring. A birthing gone bad.

He ran across the yard, hurdled a small bench and landed on Piper's steps within seconds, then pounded on the door.

A light flashed on above him. Piper looked out, saw him, heard the cow and disappeared. She reappeared on the steps seconds later, pulling on sweats over shorts as she pushed her feet into barn boots.

They took off at a run together. She unhooked the tension wire gate, shut the power down, and then re-hooked the gripping arm once Zach stepped through. The cow's mournful sound pulled them left. "Oh, Strawberry."

A red cow panted, eyes wide, her face stricken. One glance told Zach she was ready to deliver, but her strains had produced nothing. "Bad turn."

Piper examined the cow and matched his worried tone. "Should we get your father?"

Zach stripped off his shirt and shook his head. "No time. If she's been straining a while, we might have already lost the calf. You good to pull if I provide tension?"

"Yes."

"Then let's do this." He'd helped his father in the past. He knew what needed to be done. The beautiful red cow wouldn't appreciate their efforts initially, but if they could save her calf and a costly operation, he was ready to manipulate the situation. Figuratively and literally. "Okay, when she strains, I'll push. You pull."

"Gotcha."

Face down, Piper concentrated her efforts on finding limbs. The first strain produced nothing but sore arms and a frightened cow, but with the next bovine push, Zach felt something give way. "I've got movement."

"The calf?"

"I think so. I…" He cringed in pain as the cow strained to deliver her baby, then smiled. "He's alive."

"I've got a leg." The barn light gave them little glow, the cow's body shadowing their efforts, but in the dark of night, a procedure like this was primarily accomplished by memory and feel.

"And another leg!" Piper's voice hiked up as the second leg birthed, and before he could step out of the way, a last mighty strain delivered an oversize red calf onto the grass.

"A heifer."

"And pretty, like her mom," Zach added as he wiped the baby down with handfuls of dry straw. "But I'd use a different bull next time."

"I won't argue that." Piper stepped back, stared at him, then the cow and her calf, then back at him. "We're a mess."

"Nothing some soap and water won't clean up." He grinned at her as he rubbed the cow's head and neck, soothing her. "And that baby's worth it, Piper."

"Zach, thank you." She drew a deep breath, as if in apology and waved a hand toward his house. "I know this isn't why you moved here. You just wanted a nice country home, out of town, a place near hunting and fishing."

"Yup."

"And you got this. Us." She made a face. "Should I apologize? Because this wasn't exactly what you bargained for."

It wasn't.

He couldn't argue that.

Maybe he hadn't realized what he needed when he bought the split-level on Watkins Ridge, but he was pretty sure God didn't make mistakes. He planted opportunities in front of people.

He wasn't about to question why God placed him next door to Piper McKinney. They'd only met a few weeks ago, but he felt like he knew her. Or maybe it was because farming was familiar to him. He might not love farming as a career choice…

But he knew the job, the tasks at hand. And spending an hour helping Piper save a calf and a cow felt good. Life-affirming. And sometimes cops needed positive things to help balance the grim realities of their jobs. He didn't exactly deal with the cream of the crop of humanity.

He nodded toward her house once mother and baby were settled together in the foremost barn. "Your lights were on when I went by. Why were you still up?"

She sighed, scuffed a toe in the dirt, then peered up at him. "Rainey came home today."

"The twins' mother?"

"My adopted sister. That's the one."

He wanted to reach an arm out. Hug her. But he wasn't presentable enough to do that, so he held back. "How'd that go?"

"Mixed emotions on multiple fronts."

"Will she stay?"

Piper's expression said that was the question of the hour. She shrugged. "I don't know. And I don't know if I should hope she does or doesn't and that makes me feel like a loser."

"Give it time." He studied her, wishing he could be of more comfort. Crazy, convoluted families were the norm in his line of work, but seeing Piper's family stress, he realized it didn't take all that much to tip a family over the edge.

Right now, he wanted to help Piper and her family back to secure footing. Few people got to do what they loved in this life, so if part of his job on earth was to help Piper establish McKinney Farm, he'd do it.

But he knew two things: Farming was more than a career; it was a lifestyle. And he'd spent a long time thinking it was a lifestyle not meant for him.

Birthing the calf made him feel helpful. And Piper's appreciation boosted his male ego.

But how often had he prayed for his father to show up at a game? Stop by the school and watch Zach play soccer? Run track?

Marty's appearances had been infrequent. Zach wanted more than that when he settled down. He backed away from the steps and watched as Piper tiptoed inside, and when he got home he paused to check the puppies along the side of the garage.

Sweet. Sleeping. Peaceful in their little hut.

He watched quietly, not wanting to wake them. Awake, they'd long to eat and would settle for nothing else. Right now, they all could use some sleep. Including him.

But sleep eluded him for a long time. Thoughts swirled through his brain. Julia's failing marriage. Rainey's return. The twins' future. Piper's farming predicament. The town's pressure.

He'd longed for normal, all his life. A greeting-card family, gathered together.

How had fate immersed him in a real-life reality show?

Piper delivered her letter to the editor less than two hours before the *Weekly*'s deadline the following day. The middle-aged editor read the letter while Piper was there, then met Piper's gaze. "You'll make waves with this."

"Yes." Piper met the older woman's look and agreed. "I have no other choice, Aggie."

"I'm not going to edit a thing," the editor went on. "Generally I do, but I think in this case, folks will be touched by your candor. And just so you know? I'm on your side." She stared out the one small window overlooking the lake, then sighed. "I've seen a lot of things happen here in the name of progress, and I've got no problem with it most times, but this?" She set the letter down next to her laptop. "This isn't what we want for Kirkwood Lake. Tossing out the old to make way for the new. Once you step too far in that direction, there's no going back."

"I agree." Piper hesitated, wanting to say more to her mother's old friend, to ask if she ever heard from her, if she was all right? But in the end she simply shrugged. "Thanks, Aggie."

"You're welcome. And I hope folks show up in droves to that meeting. And that the supervisor's dream of a planned community gets tanked. Your family has taken enough direct hits, Piper." Aggie's eyes touched on what Piper couldn't ask. Wouldn't ask. "It's time for you to get some good breaks. Past time."

Piper couldn't disagree, but as she headed home she wondered anew at the timing of God's plan. Right now she was muddled, and the glass mirror seemed unusually fogged.

Rainey's sudden reappearance tipped her world. She'd brought trouble multiple times as a teen. Had she matured? Would things be different? Or was Piper about to take another roller-coaster ride thanks to her sister?

She pulled into the drive, parked, hooked up the manure spreader and spent the afternoon hauling nutrient-rich droppings to the fields. It was mindless work, a steady back-and-forth, necessary and mundane.

And a part of her hoped Rainey hated the smell.

Her cell phone vibrated mid-afternoon. Zach. Probably wondering why she'd gone missing for the day.

He was working the evening shift again, on the job mid-afternoon, and home after she'd be asleep for the night. And maybe that was just as well, because when he was around she couldn't imagine him *not* being around.

But right now she was surrounded by nothing but trouble, and no sane man wanted to immerse himself in that. Better she back away from those long, warm gazes. The quirk of humor. Strong, gentle hands adept at welcoming new calves and small children to his side.

No cop needed excess baggage. Inattentiveness could cost lives in crucial situations. She knew that. And it was her responsibility to draw the line in the sand. Back away from the temptation of caring for Zach. Loving him. Right now there was too much outside of her control. It wasn't Zach's fault. Or hers. Sometimes things just plain got in the way. She'd lived it enough to recognize the scenario and back off.

But she hated every minute of it.

A fire call near Interstate 86 in Clearwater kept Zach tied up most of the night. Smoke clogged the highway, making travel dangerous, and people were not pleased when he directed them to take the meandering two-lane around Kirkwood Lake. Allowing speedy traffic across smoke-filled highways wasn't going to happen on his watch.

He ignored the sour faces, and by the time the old warehouse fire had been squelched, he was dirty and smelly, and realized again why he was in love with his job.

He hadn't pulled anyone from a burning building. He hadn't put out the fire. He hadn't rescued anyone's dog.

But by manning traffic and directing folks out of harm's way, he may have saved a life.

That's why he loved wearing the uniform.

"You're a mess, Harrison."

He laughed at the commander and headed for the shower in the barracks. "Nothing that can't be washed off. For the second time today, actually."

Last night's calving seemed like a long time ago. He checked his phone once he was clean, hoping for a call from Piper.

Nothing.

He'd seen her working while he got three more deck boards installed. The pass of the tractor meant she was making work to stay away from the farm, clear of the drama, and maybe away from him?

Why?

You don't like farms, you embrace control and she's living in an uncontrolled environment that might go south at any time.

Was he that rigid?

He scrubbed a hand to the nape of his neck.

Yes.

Could he change?

Not easily. And what's more, he didn't want to change. He liked things just the way they were. Straightforward. Organized. Predictable.

A call interrupted his thoughts on the drive home. "Harrison."

"Zach, I need coverage midday tomorrow. Ozzie's out sick and Mayville's festival is going on. Can I bring you in four hours early?"

Offers of overtime had become the norm as budget cuts shut down small police forces in rural towns. Other than covering vacations, overtime used to be rare. Now? These requests had become the norm, and leaving a region shorthanded meant possibly putting someone in jeopardy. "Yes."

"And what about Monday? Just in case?"

Zach hesitated, then compromised. "Let me check things at home. I'll let you know for sure when I get to work tomorrow, but if you find someone else to take the extra, I'll step back."

"Will do."

He began the summer on a schedule, organized, planned, ready to roll.

One father, one sister, two nephews, a rotting deck, a couple of roosters and a beautiful farmer later, he was stealing moments, trying to get things done. And Zach never worked piecework. Ever. That was a big part of avoiding the farm. It wasn't the work involved, but the inconsistent drag on time, working on someone else's schedule or Mother Nature's time clock. Zach didn't do unpredictable. He liked being in charge. In control. Decisive. Anything else frustrated him.

Not seeing Piper added to that frustration, and that new wrinkle irked him even more.

Was the world changing around him? Or was he growing up enough to realize the world didn't revolve around him and his time frame?

Regardless, he had work to do, on and off the job. One way or another, he needed to get things done. Half-baked didn't work for him. Never had. Never would.

And that's just how it was.

"Aunt Piper, are you driving us to church today?" Dorrie peeked her head around the corner of the kitchen the next morning. She darted a quick look upstairs, as if afraid to be overheard.

"No." Piper leaned down and kissed Dorrie's cheek. "I'm working here today. And who put a pink ribbon in your hair?"

"My mommy." Dorrie's face said the words didn't come easily, nor the confession. "I tried to tell her I get purple and Sonya gets pink, but she said change is good."

"And it is." The ribbons were really no big thing. They just made it easier to tell the girls apart when they weren't standing together. Apart, their one-inch height difference was undetectable. "And you look beautiful no matter what color you wear."

"Thank you!" Dorrie grabbed her around the waist, hugging her. Piper lifted her up and cuddled her. The girl smelled soap-and-water clean. Her hair shone and the pink ribbon brought out tiny stripes of similar coloring in the dress she'd chosen for church. "I love you, Aunt Piper."

"Me, too!" Sonya came down the steps in her more reserved fashion, wearing the exact same bow as her sister. "I shared my pink bows with Dorrie. Doesn't she look pretty with them?"

The fact that the girls looked good in the same thing hadn't hit the twins yet. Now and again they liked to dress alike, but mostly they enjoyed being themselves. And while the world saw them as twins, they saw themselves as individuals, which meant Piper and Lucia had done something right. "You both look great in pink."

"They're beautiful, Piper."

Piper bit back a sigh. She'd been trying to sneak out the door without facing Rainey, but the girls had slowed her steps, so she faked a smile and looked up. "They look like you."

"I know." Rainey made a face that said that might not

always be a good thing, but she smiled. "We'll try to get them to make better decisions, though."

Her words screamed through Piper's brain.

Better decisions?'

Better than dragging your family's name through the mud? Than ending up unmarried and pregnant while on parole? Than abandoning twin toddlers in the dead of night?

Rainey's expression changed, which meant Piper had done a poor job of hiding her feelings. Remorse and shame shadowed Rainey's features, but then she recovered, smiled at the girls and said, "I think we're ready. Once Abuela comes down."

"Are you a good driver?" Dorrie wondered, never one to mince words.

"Yes." Rainey descended the last few stairs and faced Piper. "You're not coming?"

Her gentle tone reflected the empathy on her face, but Piper had determined she wasn't ready for a face-to-face with Rainey about much of anything yet. Right now she just wanted to be left alone. "Working. I'll pray in the fields."

Rainey's expression stayed caring, and that spiked Piper's angst. The dark-haired woman crossed the kitchen, made a cup of coffee and turned back while the coffeemaker gurgled behind her. "Ben Franklin called farming a kind and continual miracle, a reward for innocent life." She switched her attention to the hot, dry fields and breathed deep. "Although right now I expect you're not feeling too many of those miracles, Piper. I promise to do whatever I can to help you. And Mama. To be the person I should have been all along."

It was an olive branch, sincerely extended.

Rainey's face, her outer beauty, unmarked, unmarred.

Penitence softened her features and made her eyes

grayer. Deeper. She had a Madonna-like prettiness, dark and evocative, gentle and good.

But Piper refused to dive into the whys and wherefores of forgiveness now. Not here, in front of two precious girls, cast aside by the person who should always love them most. Their mother.

No olive branch or pledge of help could make that right. Not in Piper's eyes. Not when she'd suffered a similar fate. She shrugged away from the stairs, went through the back door, and headed for the feeding area.

She'd take over so Berto could go to church with his sister, niece and grandnieces. And when he grinned at the idea and hurried across the grass to clean up and accompany the family to church, Piper felt more alone than she had in years.

She watched them leave from the far side of the barn, a family, joined by love and similar coloring. Dark hair, deep eyes, latte-tinged skin.

Watching them pull away, it was Piper who felt like the outsider. A part of her wondered if that was now the case.

CHAPTER TWELVE

ZACH PULLED HIS SUV AROUND the back of Lakeside Grace and Fellowship. He parked, climbed out, then waited as his father, Julia and the boys parked directly behind him.

Julia and the kids were going on to the summer festival in Mayville. Zach was heading straight to work.

As they moved around the front of the white clapboard church, he saw Lucia and Berto bustling the twins up the stairs. Berto held one girl in his arms. Zach couldn't tell which one because they both had pink ribbons in their hair.

Lucia held firm to the other twin's hand, and her face…

Unsure, but determined, the set of her chin saying she'd face whatever proved necessary…

Was probably because of the pretty woman walking with them. Tall, slim, with thick, dark hair, the woman was an older version of the twins.

The wannabe detective in him noted two more things: Piper was nowhere to be seen, which meant she wasn't enamored of her sister's reappearance.

The *Weekly* would be delivered today, which meant the entire lakeshore would be aware of what the Kirkwood town supervisor had planned for McKinney Farm.

Would folks band together to defend farmers' rights?

Or would they go their merry way when work and play made civic duty inconvenient?

He moved up the steps, torn. He needed to be here with his family. Pray together. Form a unit. Julia needed that support around her.

But he wanted to check on Piper. See her face-to-face. Talk to her.

He'd boxed himself in with overtime today, so he wouldn't see Piper when the news hit the streets, and that was his fault, much like his father before him. Duty called. He answered. And she'd face the onslaught alone, like his mother had done, time after time. Because Marty had been that caught up in his work and it seemed like the apple hadn't fallen too far from the tree after all.

Rainey stood on the back steps when Piper came back from pouting in the fields midday. Grief slackened Rainey's jaw. Pain marked her gaze. Dorrie stood at the base of the stairs, yelling up at her mother, anger and distrust darkening her pixie features.

Rainey's expression told Piper more than words could say. She was hurting as much as anyone in this convoluted mess.

Piper choked back the bundle of mixed emotions. Years ago, her father had given her a card with one of Mother Teresa's well-known sayings: *Peace begins with a smile.*

Could it?

No way of knowing unless she tried. She hopped out of the truck, picked up Dorrie and moved toward Rainey. "Are you yelling at your mom, Dorrie?"

"I told her I don't wear pink," Dorrie screeched. Indignation hiked her voice. "I told her I wear purple and she wouldn't listen! Sonya wears pink, I wear purple and that's how it is every day!"

Piper sent a look of commiseration to Rainey, because

she looked like she could really use someone on her side. She sank to the lower step, cuddling Dorrie, and nodded for Rainey to sit. Rainey followed suit and took a seat on the step above them, to Piper's left. "You know why Abuela and I used pink for Sonya and purple for you, don't you?"

"Because those are our colors." Jaw firm, Dorrie aimed an impudent stare at her mother. "Everybody knows that!"

"Well, that's not exactly why." Piper made a face as if confessing something really big. "You and Sonya look a lot alike."

"We're twins." Dorrie rolled her eyes.

"Yes, but even identical twins have differences. You're an inch taller than your sister."

"She's short."

"Mmm-hmm." Piper sent another tiny smile toward Rainey, a look that intimated that Dorrie might be the most like her mother.

And Rainey aimed a ghost of a smile back, understanding.

"But you have different natures. Sonya is more cautious."

"I'm not afraid of anything," Dorrie boasted.

"And you're more hotheaded."

"Sonya's nicer."

"I'd say more easygoing. Eager to please," Piper replied. "So the reason we use the different ribbons is because Abuela and I need to be able to tell you apart when we see you, but God gives a very special gift to mothers. They can always tell their twins apart."

"No, they can't."

"Yes, they can." Rainey moved down to their level. "From the time you were born I could tell you apart in an instant. Others couldn't. But I could. And I still can, Doralia."

"Then why'd you leave?" Dorrie stared right at her

mother and asked the million-dollar question they'd all been waiting to have answered. "If you can tell us apart so well, you must love us, but if mommies love their little girls, they don't leave them. Right, Aunt Piper?"

Piper swallowed a rock-sized lump in her throat, working to push aside memories of a ten-year-old girl whose mother left.

Had Nina McKinney cared? Even a little?

No, or she'd have come back. Called. Written. Sent cards.

But this conversation wasn't about her, it was about Rainey, Sonya and Dorrie. "Dorrie, I wish I could give you answers off the top of my head, but sometimes adults do things because they think they're right at the time."

Rainey's gaze shot to hers, and her eyes—questing, searching Piper's—said Piper was onto something. So Rainey had left because of something or someone.

"The important thing is that Mommy's here now. She came back to help take care of you guys."

"And help on the farm." Rainey met her gaze, unflinching. "Whatever it takes, Piper."

Piper appreciated the promise of help, but she wasn't much different from Dorrie. Could she trust Rainey? Had she matured enough to face life, day by day, without running away?

The smile, remember?

She turned her attention up to Rainey and offered a genuine smile, a look that said sisters should stick together.

Rainey's gaze grew moist.

Her chin quivered, as if she felt undeserving.

A bird chirped above them, followed by another. Not the quaint song of the cautious oriole, but the clear trill of the finch, joyous and free.

"So, Dorrie." Piper stood, dusted off the seat of her pants and handed the pink ribbon to Dorrie. "I don't think Mommy cares what color ribbon you wear, but she doesn't need a daily argument over it. Got it? And we don't yell at grown-ups. Ever."

"Okay. Sorry." Dorrie aimed a not-really-sorry look her mother's way, chin firm, lower lip thrust out.

"Your lack of sincerity is appalling." Piper stepped back and pointed, keeping her voice firm. "Apologize to your mother nicely, and then let's get some lunch. I'm starving."

"Is Trooper Zach coming over?"

"No." Piper replied as if it was no big deal that Zach wasn't around today, but it felt like a big deal. It felt like he'd noted the craziness of the McKinney clan and bowed out, quietly. Which was exactly what she thought he should do, so why did it hurt so much?

The sound of Zach's name and title made Rainey pale.

And that confirmed the thought Zach put in Piper's mind. Rainey had run scared three years ago.

Given time, she might just tell them from whom. Or what.

Piper's phone rang just then. She saw Zach's name and answered it. They were neighbors, after all. And avoidance could only go so far. "Hey. Are you at work already?"

"I am. Overtime. Again."

"I wondered when I saw your car pull out…well, actually I wondered more when it didn't come back." She cringed, wishing she could snatch the words back.

Too late. "You were watching for me."

"Was not. Just working and happened to notice."

"You weren't in church this morning."

"No." She hesitated while Rainey and Dorrie went inside. "I decided I'd be like those birds you're so fond of. Talk to God in the fields."

"I saw the family there."

Rainey's family. Not hers.

"I figured you were home, pouting."

The accuracy of that put her back up, but before she could come up with a suitable retort, he laughed and said, "I'm ordering Chinese food to be delivered for all of you later."

"You're... What? Why would you do that?"

"Because your article is creating a furor in town, you're going to be inundated with people today both in person and on the phone, and I wanted to help even though I'm working."

"Zach, that's nice, but..." She started to put him off, but then noticed the line of cars pulling into the farm drive.

And twice her phone signaled that people were calling her while she talked to Zach. "There are people pulling in right now. Some I know. Some I don't."

"Go. Talk to them. And hang tight. Remember you've got my father there to help, so work the crowd. Do what you can. I'm only sorry I won't be there to offer assistance. Consider supper my contribution."

His words touched her heart, but she understood and respected why he'd left the family farm. Not everyone was wired to embrace Mother Nature.

She was.

He wasn't.

End of story.

"What's going on?" Rainey came back outside and moved closer to Piper in a gesture of unity that felt good and strange all at once as the stream of cars continued.

"The town is trying to seize part of the farm."

"They're what?" Rainey's scowl said more than her growled words. "Over my dead body."

"My thoughts exactly," Piper replied, and it felt funny to actually be talking with Rainey, much less agreeing with her. "But we'll have a fight on our hands this week.

You up for it?" She faced Rainey. "Because it might not be pretty, Rain."

"Prison wasn't pretty." Rainey shrugged shoulders that appeared delicate, but the grit in her voice said she was anything but. "This? A walk in the park, Piper."

"That's what I was hoping to hear." They walked down the stairs as local people climbed out of their cars. People from all over the area stopped by, wondering what was going on and pledging their support.

The phone rang continually.

More folks came by, unannounced.

And through it all, Rainey stood sentinel by Piper's side, determination marking her jaw. A part of Piper wondered how Rainey would feel once she heard the price offered for the farm. Would her cut of seven figures make her reconsider her position?

Piper hoped not, but promised cash was seductive when you were low on funds, and Piper was pretty sure Rainey was broke.

At least Chas and Colin hadn't gotten to her yet, but Piper knew her brothers well. They would.

CHAPTER THIRTEEN

"HARRISON. MY OFFICE."

When the shift commander spoke, smart guys listened. Zach followed the captain into his office and shut the door. "Yes, sir?"

The captain nodded to a chair.

Zach sat.

The captain slid a document across his desk.

Zach picked it up, read the recommendation, and grinned. "I appreciate this, sir. Very much."

"Your work is commendable." The captain dipped his gaze to the paper clutched in Zach's hand. "This is two years overdue, but we were caught in budget constraints for a while. With more area to cover, we need more competent investigators. Congratulations, Zach."

He stood.

So did Zach.

This promotion was something he'd hoped for. Planned for. The raise in pay was nothing to take lightly, but the compliment from his commanders and the possibility to then move into a sergeant's position spoke volumes.

He was on an upward climb, just as he'd anticipated. It may have taken longer than he thought, but he'd been tapped, finally.

It felt great.

The first thing he did when the shift commander

released him was call Piper. He knew she'd be busy, but he needed to share his great news.

A promotion.

Fewer nights, most likely.

The idea of being home at night made him smile. Being home at night with a certain farmer?

Better yet.

Would she answer the phone? Was she tied up with people coming to aid her cause? He hated not knowing what was going on, but when she answered in her typical style, nothing else mattered. "Aren't you supposed to be working?"

He laughed. "Kind of. But I had to call you. I just got promoted."

"Zach!" Her voice tipped up, delighted. "That's wonderful news! I'm so happy for you, this is what you wanted. What you've been working for! Congratulations!"

She sounded as happy as he felt and that made him happier, if such a thing was possible. "I can't talk because we're rolling, but I had to call and tell you first thing."

"You called me first?"

This time he laughed. "Yes. Next call is my father."

"Oh, Zach."

"Gotta run."

"I'm so proud of you."

Pride shimmered in her voice, and he'd forgotten how nice it felt to have someone be proud of him. His goals. His accomplishments. "Thanks, Piper."

She sighed, the tiny sound making him long to hold her. Dream of a future together. "You're welcome."

"I'd like to work in the dairy store," Rainey announced as the adults helped themselves to Chinese food that evening. "Noreen can't handle a full-time position. Jen and Ada are leaving for college in twelve days and I'm here. If Marly is willing to keep her hours as they are, why don't I cover the dairy store in exchange for room and board?"

"This is a good idea, no?" Berto gazed straight at Piper as if hoping she'd agree.

Lucia hummed softly, her face concerned.

Intent, Marty ate lo mein while watching the conversation unfold. Julia and the kids had taken their plates to the picnic tables outside, so the adults could speak freely after a busy day of networking with half the town.

Piper shook her head. "Um, no. First of all, you're family, and the idea of family paying room and board to be a productive member of a working farm is ludicrous. Second, you need a paycheck like the rest of us. The dairy is self-supporting, so while we can't float you benefits yet, we can pay you fourteen dollars an hour. If you love running the dairy and can take over as manager at some time, we'll figure out a different pay scale."

"Piper, I didn't mean to—"

"Third…" Piper shushed Rainey's argument with a pointed look. "I have spent the last year asking God for help. I've begged, cajoled, berated and whined, and all the while I thought I was asking for more money in the bank. Fewer bills. Rain in the fields."

The group nodded collectively.

Piper pointed around the room. "What I got was Marty. And now you. That right there is the answer to prayer as far as I'm concerned. Lucia and I were just trying to figure out how to run the store once Ada and Jen go back to school, manage the girls, help out with their school projects, run the farm…" She raised her glass higher. "To us. And to the continued success of McKinney Farm. I'm grateful that each of you is here and on our side because we know we have a fight on our hands."

"Hear, hear!" Berto smiled and raised his coffee mug.

Lucia's face softened in approval.

Julia poked her head in the door. "I'm taking these guys home to bed. They're zonked. The twins are insisting on five more minutes of swinging."

"Of course they are." Rainey went outside to gather the girls once their five minutes were up.

"I'll help, Julia." Marty tossed his paper plate into the recycling bag and turned toward Piper. "You keep the faith over here. You've got lots of folks on your side, so don't get down over this whole thing."

"I won't," she promised, then gave him a spontaneous hug. "Thank you. For everything."

"You've got it backward, Piper. It's me who should be thanking you. Letting me work here. Giving me a chance. That's the best therapy I could ask for."

"Glad to help." Piper made a face to Julia as Marty strode toward his grandsons, whistling. "You get what a godsend he's been to us, right? What a treasure? His help, his strength, his expertise. Your father's amazing."

"Tri-Central Dairy was a well-run enterprise," Julia agreed. "He learned from the best and applied it daily."

"Tri-Central?" The name of one of the most renowned New York dairy farms stopped Piper in her tracks. "Marty *owned* Tri-Central?"

"Yes."

Piper stared after the tall man walking away from them. "He's like the dairy king of New York State. The mastermind of three milkings a day, rapid pasturing, and the integrated computer program that charts each cow's daily production."

"Neat, huh? He set a lot of protocol with his innovations."

"Not neat," Piper corrected her. "Mind-boggling. Intimidating. Possibly earth-shattering."

Julia laughed, but shook her head. "Dad would feel bad if he thought he made you nervous."

Making Marty feel bad was the last thing she wanted, but knowing he'd owned one of the most productive and successful farming enterprises in the Northeast knocked her heart out of rhythm.

Did he consider her inept?

Memories of ag school videos about Tri-Central filled her brain. Marty was the guy authors cited when illustrating success.

She was the kind of farmer they ignored as inconsequential.

What must he think of their antiquated methods? Their penny-pinching ways? The trail of debt she'd worked so hard to pay down?

"See you tomorrow." Julia waved a hand as she followed her father and the boys. "We did well today, Piper."

They had.

They'd witnessed an outpouring of support. Some offered time, some pledged money, many offered both. Of the dozens she'd talked with today, no one wanted to see Palmeteer succeed in his quest to change their town this radically.

And they all promised to show up to Thursday's meeting.

By the time Rainey and Lucia got the girls to bed, Piper had the kitchen straightened up. A cool breeze pulled her outside, a respite from the hot days. Lucia followed. Then Rainey. Berto blamed his early milking hour and had gone to bed.

Piper should do the same, but she wanted a little down time, letting the cooler breeze wash over her. "This feels wonderful."

"Yes."

"*Si.*" Lucia smiled at both young women. "And it is nice to be with you both. At last."

Rainey's face said it might not be as nice as her mother supposed. "I have to talk to you. To both of you. And

I'm not sure how to say all this, but you need to know everything before you offer me a job and a home."

Lucia's chin tightened. Her gaze shadowed. But her firm nod said she knew this was coming. "There is nothing you need to hide from us. Ever, my daughter."

Piper couldn't be quite as sure, but she nodded agreement.

"I broke my parole years ago."

Lucia frowned. "You didn't. I was here, the whole time."

Piper didn't believe it either. "When? I don't remember you doing a thing wrong."

Rainey made a face. Her long fingers gripped the table's edge. "First let me say this: I never held up that convenience store."

Piper shifted, uncomfortable, because while most people proclaimed their innocence, the majority of convicted felons were guilty. Regardless of what they said.

Lucia showed no such hesitation. "I knew this."

"Thank you, Mama, but I *was* in the car. I didn't know what was going down because I'd been drinking." She made a face of self-disgust, then faced them both again. "When I realized what they'd done, I took the fall because Chloe was pregnant. I was a year younger and I'd heard what happens in women's prisons and I thought I'd get juvie time. That way I could save her baby from being born in prison."

"But you were charged as an adult," Lucia exclaimed. "Why did you not explain yourself then?"

"I thought I was saving a friend. A baby. I thought if I did the eighteen months, then Chloe would be able to have her baby and he or she would have a chance to be normal."

"And?"

"She didn't continue the pregnancy," Rainey told them. Her face went grim. "She sent me fake pictures of a little boy she called Brian. She led me along the entire time so that I would keep her secret. And others helped, pretending she was doing well with her baby on the West Coast. That I had done a brave and noble thing."

"Oh, Larraina." Lucia gripped her daughter's hands. "You put your heart and trust in the wrong people, my child."

"I know that now. I didn't know that then. So I went to prison and…" Her face paled. Memories made her shoulders shudder. "I dealt with all the terrible things prison had to offer. But I survived, determined to be a good person once I got out."

"And you were." Piper leaned forward. "What happened?"

"I found out what Chloe had done. What my supposed friends had done. And I went out drinking. You were gone." She looked at Lucia. "Aunt Ana was sick and you went to Mexico to see her one last time."

"Ana Rosa. Yes."

"And you." She re-centered her gaze on Piper. "You were crazy busy because your father had died and you were trying to run the farm on your own and go to school."

Piper remembered well. "It was a rough time, all right."

"I met an old classmate the night I found out about Chloe's deception. We drank too much. We spent the night together. My anger and disappointment was no excuse for my actions, I know that now, but it produced my two wonderful daughters, and I thank God for them. But Hunter saw me that night."

Piper's heart seized.

"He was there, with a girl."

At a bar with a girl while he was dating Piper. She bit back a pang of disappointment. Young. Stupid. Naive. Much as Rainey had been.

"I didn't know this for a long time, but later, after the twins were born, I saw him as I went to a therapy session at the mental health clinic in Clearwater. He was meeting with bad people. It was almost dark, midwinter, and there was no place to park so I had to circle the block slowly, looking for a spot. He saw me. And he knew I saw him, even though they were just stepping out of a crack joint, into the shadows. He threatened to go to the police and my parole officer. He said he used his cell phone to make a video of me, drinking two years before. My parole did not allow drinking and he knew he could send me back to jail. And he reminded me of the ugly things that happen to girls in jail. And how he would then marry Piper and be a guardian to my girls."

Piper sucked a breath. Lucia blessed herself as tears slipped down her brown, weathered cheeks.

"I ran. I knew the girls would be safe with you two, and I couldn't go back to prison. But I couldn't let Hunter go free. I couldn't let you marry him or let him near my girls, so I called the police department and gave them a tip. Then the state police. And then the district attorney's office. There was no way of knowing who was honest and who was not, but I knew one of them would take it seriously."

"And then you ran."

She nodded, ashamed. "I hid for three long years, not daring to show my face. Praying the girls were safe and that you would not hate me for leaving. And praying I would not be found and sent back to prison for breaking parole."

"But you've come back," Piper said softly. "Because?"

"I will no longer live in fear," Rainey explained. "I won't let evil make my choices for me. I will face what needs to be faced as an adult. As a mother my children will look up to one day. I came back because I need to reclaim my life. God has forgiven my iniquities. He has washed me clean. But I must face what is coming to me."

"Oh, Rainey."

"Why must you?" her mother asked, distraught. "It is over now. It is in the past. Why must we bring it up now?"

"Because you raised me to do the right thing, always," she told her mother. "And with the birth of my girls I have done so, except for this. Now I must make amends and do as the courts instruct me to do. I am just sorry for all the stupid things I've done."

Lucia waved that off. "Many are stupid when young. Time gives us wisdom, wisdom you've found. Do you have to do this thing? Confess one night of drinking?"

"I must." Rainey raised a gentle hand to her mother's weathered skin. "You know this. We all know this." She directed her gaze to include Piper. "If they send me back to jail, I must ask you to watch over Dorrie and Sonya for whatever time I am gone. But then I will come back and take my place as your daughter—" she faced her mother "—and your sister—" she turned toward Piper "—if you will have me."

She'd sacrificed eighteen months for a lying, cheating friend.

She'd been lied to, humiliated and suffered indignities of prison life.

She'd tried to put things right and fell short for one night. One foolish, wretched night, out of hundreds? Thousands?

Should anyone go back to prison for drinking one night?

Piper's heart rose up to choke her.

Rainey was a convicted felon who broke parole.

Zach was a newly promoted investigator.

How would that look to his boss? His commanders? How would they see this whole thing playing out? A police investigator taking up with a woman who had a relationship with a crooked cop...and now housing a parole-breaking felon.

How could she do this to him? How could she fix this, make it right?

She couldn't. But she couldn't cast Rainey out, either, because she saw the truth she'd missed years ago. Rainey's sacrificial spirit pushed her to take the blame for something she didn't do, and then suffer the consequences. Piper had doubted then, ready to believe the worst. And Rainey suffered.

Rainey didn't deserve to endure any more.

And she couldn't justify dragging Zach down, churning in the muck surrounding her.

So be it. They'd made bad choices while young, but that stopped here and now. She could save Zach by cutting him loose. Setting him free.

He'd still be a neighbor.

But at least he wouldn't be tainted by the smudge of lawlessness that surrounded her family.

Rainey had come home. The truth could set her free but also lock her up. No matter what, Piper and Lucia would be there for her because they were family, joined not by blood but love.

Heartsick, she stood, rounded the table and hugged Rainey. "I will help you in any way I can, but you have to promise us to never run again. If you must come clean, you will tell the whole truth, including Chloe's deception."

"That's over now. Revealing that cannot help anything."

"We don't know that," Piper argued. "But I know one thing: we women will stick together from now on. And that's a promise."

She went inside, holding back tears until she climbed into bed.

Rainey's sacrifice had gone unrewarded.

She'd suffered.

Her words showed a side of her Piper hadn't seen before, but they also dictated the actions Piper must take.

A new investigator couldn't afford to have his reputation sullied. She had to make sure that didn't happen. Shunning him would break her heart, but she had no other choice. Not if she truly loved him.

She'd realized that when he'd helped her bring a sweet red calf into the world, unharmed. She loved the big guy, heart and soul.

And now she had to give him up.

CHAPTER FOURTEEN

Z ACH EYED THE UNFINISHED DECK and Piper's farm the next morning, mulling his options, then he set off across the yard at a quick clip. "Hey."

Piper turned quickly, but not so fast that he didn't see the pain in her eyes. When she swung back his way, it was gone, and for just a moment he wondered if he saw it at all, but Zach was quick on the uptake. Something put that in her eyes. Or someone. He needed to know who.

"Good morning, Investigator."

He smiled. "It sounds good, right?"

"Excellent." She sent him a pert smile that didn't reach her eyes and finished lacing her work boot.

"I was hoping we could celebrate tomorrow."

She made a face at him and started walking toward the John Deere. "I'm tied up this week. Maybe you could celebrate with your dad and Julia."

A not-too-subtle brush-off. He wanted to wave it off as nerves, but his heart told him otherwise and his senses rarely misled him. "What's going on, Piper?"

"Nothing." Face flat, she faced him as she started to climb aboard the tractor. "You know how farming is, Zach. I'm just crazy busy right now. And I've got a lot going on." She jutted her chin toward the house and dairy. "But we're all truly happy for you. The whole neighborhood will be thrilled to have their very own investigator on hand."

"You're upset."

She shook her head. "Not at all."

"But you're treating me like I'm just another neighbor."

She stared right at him. And in that moment he knew that was the very message she wanted to send. They were neighbors with two property lines in common and that was that.

His heart slowed. His breathing did, too.

Because when he'd talked with her eighteen hours ago she sounded normal. Happy for him and with him. So what messed that up?

She tapped her phone. "I've got to get going. I heard your sister has an interview this afternoon. Wish her well for me. I hope they grab her and you guys can have a double reason to celebrate."

"Yeah. Thanks."

She started the engine, gave him a friendly wave, shoved the big rig into gear and rolled toward the back cattle barn.

He stared after her, trying to reason things out, and got nothing.

She was under a lot of pressure. Surrounded by emotional situations between her sister's return and her brothers' animosity.

He'd give her time. Cut her some slack. And track her down again in a few hours. She probably just needed breathing room.

He called her just after twelve noon.

No answer.

He tried again before going in to work.

Same result.

If he had time he'd find her and extract the truth, but what if the truth was nothing he wanted to hear? What if she just plain didn't care? How dumb would he look?

You're afraid to look stupid? It's time to grovel. Get with the program or you'll never get the girl.

He kicked the tire on his SUV, left the puppies for someone else to handle because tiny, sweet, baby creatures only frustrated him right now, and went to work, a lot less happy than he'd been twenty-four hours ago.

Two days of no contact.

That was forty-seven hours too long for Zach, and he was determined to have a face-to-face with Piper by Wednesday night. One way or another he'd find out what went wrong and fix it.

His father had been running countless errands the past several days.

His sister had landed the job with a local OB practice and would move here permanently in three weeks. His nephews were excited about living near the twins, and he couldn't argue the fact that a certain McKinney fascinated him, too.

Except she was stonewalling him and wouldn't say why. He crossed the yard, went up the steps and knocked on their back door.

"Zach." Lucia answered the door. "Piper is not here."

"Yes, she is."

Lucia's expression said whether she was or wasn't didn't matter. Piper McKinney wasn't available to talk to him. Period.

"Tell her I'm not leaving until we talk."

Lucia acknowledged his words with little expression. "I will pass along your information. When she returns."

She dipped her gaze south. At the tip of the farm lane, Zach caught sight of the big blue New Holland tractor lumbering down the hill. "My father got it running."

"Like new. He is very good at machines. Piper is fertilizing the cornfields on the county road. Rain is forecast. Maybe this time they will be correct."

The forecast might be right this time, Zach thought. Clouds, dense and dark, had been gathering over Lake Erie. A west wind would push them up and away. But a quirk to the northwest would bring them right here, with the promise of a daylong rain.

A rain that would ease worry for a lot of folks. It wouldn't be fair to bother her now, but he wouldn't be put off much longer. Not when so much was at stake.

He didn't make promises lightly. Neither did Piper. A man knew these things about the woman he longed to make his wife. The mother of his children. No matter how long he'd known her.

Rainey came down the steps at a quick clip as he turned to go. "The girls are asleep and I'm heading to the dairy."

Lucia sent her a look, an expression he remembered from that first meeting weeks ago.

Nervous. Mistrustful. Uneasy in his presence.

Which meant Rainey's arrival had changed things. Determined, Zach turned on his heel and left. Piper might be maintaining a vow of silence. She might be giving him the cold shoulder. But he was a cop and if Rainey's reappearance put his life in a tailspin, he'd find out why.

Moose Braeburn's number popped up in Piper's phone as she angled the tractor out of the first cornfield. "Moose. What's up?"

"I've got news, Piper. Big news. The kind of thing your father and I prayed for. It's here, finally."

Piper's mind went straight to the town controversy. "About Palmeteer and his buddies trying to take over the world as we know it?"

Moose laughed. "No. We'll show them who runs this town Thursday night. This is different. I'm across the lake at the Elliots' place. I can be your way in five. Where are you?"

"On County Road 18 side-dressing corn. Meet me here."

"Done."

Piper's mind ran in several directions as she watched Moose's pickup turn into the farm lane. She swung down from the tractor and headed his way. "I can't imagine what's got you this wound up. Did you and Ginny win the lottery?"

He shook his head. "No, ma'am. Money comes too hard to let it go that freely. No, this is better. Much better."

She made a face and lifted her shoulders. "I've got nothin'. Tell me."

He held out an official-looking document. Piper scanned it quickly, then went back and read more carefully. "They're building a new Greek yogurt facility between here and I-90?"

"And they want our milk," Moose exclaimed.

This *was* a dream come true. To make Greek-style yogurt, workers double-pressed pasteurized milk, making the end result thicker and drier. Fewer calories, higher protein, Greek-style yogurt had become the "it food" of the moment, and the chance they'd collectively prayed for.

Pressing required four times the milk needed for ordinary yogurt. That meant the manufacturing plant needed local milk for optimum profitability. Which meant she could drive her milk production up and stay in business. If she could defeat the town and keep her farm. "When did they approach you?"

"Friday. We had Diana's wedding on Saturday, or I'd have gotten the word out sooner. Then your news about the town broke on Sunday, and that's all anyone could talk about. I wanted to talk to you alone. Get you in on the ground floor. Your daddy and I knew farming would pay off one day. The right time, right product, right place. This is it, Piper. This is that day."

Moose's words reflected her father's beliefs. He'd prayed for that very thing. During every hard time Tucker McKinney shrugged his shoulders and reminded everyone that good things happen to those who wait on the Lord.

Chas and Colin got tired of waiting long ago. Not Piper. She'd always believed.

She hugged Moose, then stepped back. "Do you want to tell Berto and Lucia with me?"

"No time." He moved toward his pickup, more relaxed than she'd ever seen him. "I promised them figures by next Tuesday. We're meeting tonight at my place. Come see what things look like in black and white. What kind of production numbers we need to have. And then tomorrow night we'll face down the town together. All of us."

Not all of them. After pushing Zach aside the past three days, she was pretty sure he'd be a no-show. And she couldn't blame him.

"I'll be there," she promised. "What time?"

"Seven."

Perfect. Zach was off tonight. If she was gone, he couldn't track her down. Wrangle the truth out of her.

She thought it would be hard to shrug him off. Turn her back. Go about her business as if he were any old guy.

She didn't know it would be impossible.

"What did Moose want?" Lucia looked up as Piper entered the kitchen once she finished the second field. "He called here looking for you, then said he'd try your cell. He sounded anxious."

"Not anxious. Happy. If we're willing to work together, we could have a milk contract in place by October. A contract that offers top dollar for all the milk we can produce."

"God be praised, this is what we've been hoping for, Piper!" Lucia grabbed her into a big hug, then twirled her around the room. "A contract for more milk, guaranteed. How happy you must be! For this, your father dreamed and planned many years. And now we see his dream come true. You. Me. Berto. Why are you not more happy?"

Piper shrugged. "I want to be thrilled. But what if tomorrow night doesn't go our way? What if Palmeteer gets his way and makes our land town property? No matter how they reimburse us, once land is gone, it's gone. And every time I look downhill, I see my heritage. I see my grandparents and great-grandparents, carving this place out of dense forest. I don't want to give that up, no matter what the supervisor thinks is best. Or how much they pay."

"And there is the matter of the policeman next door."

Tears pricked Piper's eyes. She blinked them back and turned away, but Lucia moved closer. "You worry that if you care for him, it will hurt him. That your family will be bad for him."

"No." Piper bit her lip and grabbed a wad of tissues. "Well. Maybe. But if life's a jigsaw puzzle, we've got some weird pieces on the table, and sometimes you just can't make them fit. And that's how it is with Zach."

"Does he fit you?"

"Well, yes, but—"

"Then nothing else is of consequence."

How Piper wished that was true. "Life doesn't come with carefully orchestrated happily ever afters."

"It does for those who embrace God's plan. You think too much, Piper. Always you think, you plan, you schedule, but then you are thwarted by rain or snow or illness and you get angry. A plan is better written in sand than stone. That way it can be adjusted with greater ease."

"You think I should tell Zach about Rainey."

Lucia stared out the window. The slanted light backlit her concern, but brightened her eyes. "I think in this case it might be good to have a friend who knows police things. A person we can trust."

Piper couldn't imagine anyone more trustworthy than Zach, but telling him…that meant they'd have to face decisions immediately. Was Rainey ready for that? Were they?

"He was here before. Looking for you. He said he will not stop until he speaks with you."

Three days of avoiding him showed her the foolishness of her actions. How many times a day did her eyes dart to his home?

More than she could count.

How often did her hand reach for the phone?

Constantly.

She sighed and looked west. Dishonesty didn't sit well with her. While she watched, Zach came out of his house, his tool belt slung around blue-jean-wrapped hips, topped by a smudged white T-shirt that said he'd been working on the half-finished deck.

Hands in her pockets, she pushed through the screen door, chin down, longing to see him, hating confrontation. But Lucia was right. Honesty was always the best policy and she was foolish to think otherwise.

Piper was heading his way.

Zach's heart tripped in his chest.

His hands itched to gather her in and promise everything would be all right, except he couldn't make rash promises. Not as a man, not as a cop. But right now he wanted to do whatever he could to put joy back in her step. To see a smile that touched her eyes when they met his. Her gaze said they had a long way to go.

He straightened, folded his arms and angled his head. "You finally decided to talk to me."

She indicated the picnic table under the tree with a thrust of her head. "Can we sit?"

"Sure."

She sank onto the seat, studied the deck and sent him a look of appreciation. "It's coming along. And it's beautiful, Zach. I knew it would be."

"I've had plenty of time to work on it these past few days," he reminded her.

She flushed, her eyes cast downward, then shrugged. "We need to talk."

"So I gathered."

He hadn't meant it to sound so cryptic, but when she flashed him a heated look he realized that maybe shaking her out of her emotional funk wasn't a bad thing. He held up a hand and ticked off his fingers. "You wouldn't talk with me, celebrate with me, answer my calls or acknowledge my presence on the planet. Yeah. I'd say we're overdue for a conversation."

She hesitated.

A part of him longed to help. Another part wanted to shake sense into her. A true heart was nothing to be taken lightly, and she should know that better than most after dealing with Reilich's duplicity.

"You're a great guy, Zach."

"That's the line women use when they want to let a guy down easy. Cut to the chase, Piper."

His tough voice put her back up and it heartened him to see it. "I don't use lines, Zach. I don't mince words and I don't play with people's feelings. Ever."

"Could have fooled me."

"Which is why I'm over here, you big lug," she stormed. He couldn't deny it made him feel good to see that sizzle in her gaze. "If you'd just keep your comments to a minimum, I might be able to explain myself."

He didn't dare smile outwardly, but inwardly?

Joy eclipsed pain.

Her little tirade said more than any explanation could. Her look? Her angst? Her quick reply?

Said he mattered. A lot. And that's what he was hoping to find out. "Go on. Please."

She made a face and sent him a look, then shrugged. "My family has issues."

"Don't they all."

"Mine go beyond emotional and financial. Mine go to criminal."

"Rainey."

"Yes."

He met her gaze head-on. "Tell me what she's done, and then explain why you didn't come to me right away. I may be a cop but I'm also a guy who knows the system. I get help for people every single day. It's what I do, Piper."

"She broke parole."

"She's not on parole," Zach noted. "That was years ago."

"She broke it then. She found out she'd been double-crossed and that the girl she took a rap for didn't really have a kid and so she went out drinking and Hunter saw her and used it to blackmail her later."

"Let's back up slowly. What do you mean, Rainey took a rap for someone?"

"She didn't hold up that convenience store."

"You're sure about that?" Years of experience put doubt in his voice.

Piper nodded. "Yes. The girl who robbed the place was pregnant and Rainey took the heat off of her, figuring she'd get charged as a juvenile."

"She didn't."

"No. But she still didn't tell because she didn't want Chloe to be pregnant in prison. But then Chloe terminated the pregnancy and pretended to have a kid so Rainey would take the heat."

"Why would anyone give up part of their life to do that?"

Piper's expression said she wondered the same thing, but then she shrugged. "Because she's Rainey. She's got a sacrificial nature. She thought she was saving a friend. And the friend's baby."

"But why would Reilich blackmail her? What was in it for him?"

"She saw him at a shakedown with his crooked friends. And he saw her."

Now things were starting to make sense. Reilich had a lot at stake back then. Rainey was lucky they didn't just put a hit out on her and be done with it. Reilich loved power. That lust for control had done him in. "So she ran."

Piper nodded. "Yes. But she's tired of running so she's come back. And before she left town she called in tips to multiple agencies, wanting to get Hunter and his gang off the streets."

"You're telling me Rainey was the informant?"

"Yes."

"Oh, man." He scrubbed a hand to his jaw and stared at her, mystified. "Do you know how much she helped with those calls?"

Piper shook her head.

"She named four separate men that she recognized. She gave the date and time so their presence could be verified. The investigators tracked their cell phones to back up her assertions. Those phone calls gave them hard, fast evidence of the meeting. A street camera gave additional info. And the timing fit with a major drug score outside Buffalo, which meant they were involved. Her phone calls didn't just set up the investigation, they nailed it for the prosecution. But she used a burner phone and no one could ID the caller."

"She was scared."

"And rightfully so," Zach told her. "Those guys played for keeps and killing a witness wouldn't have made them lose any sleep. So she's worried about the night she broke parole and went out drinking?"

"Yes." Piper leaned forward, earnest. "But she's willing to do whatever it takes to fix things. She realizes her choices will mess up the girls' future. So she wants to come clean and do her time now. But we don't know how to do that and I didn't want your bosses to think you're bad or crooked or just plain stupid for being involved with a woman who already had a reputation with a bad cop. And now has a felon living under her roof."

"That's all?"

She frowned as if he were deaf. "Don't get smart with me, Zach. You just got handed a well-deserved promotion. I won't be responsible for ruining your career. End of story."

It wasn't the end of the story at all, but he let that pass for the moment. "You avoided me to save me?"

"Well. Yes."

"Because you care that much?"

No way could she gaze into his eyes, hear the gentle rumble of his voice and pretend not to care. "Yes."

He stood and drew himself up to his full height, then reached down and pulled her up too. "Do I look like I need saving?"

"Zach, I—"

"Or like I can't make up my own mind about who to love? How to spend my days?"

"Zach, we—"

He hushed her with a kiss. He was done with words. Done with explanations. Done with anything that pulled them apart. When he finally drew back, he cradled her face between his two broad hands and smiled at her.

"How did you think you'd avoid me, Piper? I live next door."

"That part of my plan fell apart about an hour into it," she admitted. "I couldn't stop thinking about you. Wanting to see you." She let her gaze drop to his mouth. "Kiss you."

"Glad to oblige," he whispered as his lips found hers again. "And the next time you assume you're going to ruin my life, fill me in ahead of time, okay? It's so much more fun to mess things up together."

At that moment, with his lips against hers, she couldn't disagree.

When he drew back, smiling, he tweaked her nose. "Kissing you is preferable to not kissing you. Keep that in mind for future reference."

"Speaking of the future." She worried her lip and shifted topics. "If we succeed in making the town back down tomorrow night, you'll have one more reason to want to walk away from me and possibly never look back."

"Our proximity makes that improbable and my feelings make it impossible, but spill it. What else could you possibly hit me with today?"

"Yogurt." She laid out Moose's information for Zach. "That means more work. More farm. More cows. Basically everything you ran from."

He mulled that as his father stepped out of the milking parlor. "I think God does that on purpose sometimes. To teach us a lesson. And I'm not foolish enough to think that being in love with a cop is easy business. There's a level of concern that goes higher when you're on the force, but you never scold about that."

"Because you love what you do," she told him.

Her sincerity deepened his smile.

"When you love someone, you try to support them. What they do, what they love. It's not my job to change you." She shrugged, honest to the core. "And the fact that you're totally hot in the uniform buys you serious points."

"Good to hear." The warmth of his smile shifted her world back into focus. "You put up with the downsides of loving a guy with a badge. I'll deal with the farm stuff. But right now," he released her as his father drew closer, "Dad and I have an errand to run."

"And I interrupted your deck work again."

"Do you see me complaining?"

His tone made her smile. "No." A buzz pulled her attention to her phone. She read the text and waved toward the farm. "There's a reporter waiting for me. Wish me well."

"You'll be fine," he told her. He reached out and gave her a quick hug, enough to bolster her confidence. "I'll call you later. Maybe we can get ice cream after your meeting."

"Quietly?"

"Not around here."

She laughed and it felt good to laugh. She'd laid a lot at his door, but he hadn't flinched.

He'd taken charge. As she crossed the field to meet with the local reporter, she considered Lucia's advice. She'd risked Rainey's balance to make Piper happy. And she'd put her trust in Zach to guide them.

That meant a great deal to Piper.

"You sure you've got time to come with me?" Marty asked as he and Zach moved to the SUV a half hour later. "I know you want to get the deck done."

"The wood's not going anyplace," Zach told him.

Marty sent him a look of disbelief. "A little out of character, aren't you?"

His tone inspired Zach's smile. "For the moment. I'm trying to learn to go with the flow more."

Marty made a face as he climbed into the passenger side. "Not an easy lesson for guys like you and me. Have you seen Julia today?"

Zach shook his head as he angled the SUV west toward Vince and Linda's place. "No. Why?"

"She's heading back to Ithaca on Friday to take care of the house. Get things packed. I told her we'd keep the boys here."

His father? Watching kids? Zach couldn't react in time to hide his surprise. "You're okay with that? Really?"

His father's expression changed. A quiet shadow stilled his gaze, but then he hiked a brow and turned to face Zach. "I'm good with kids."

Zach hadn't known that. Not personally. And yet, his father handled Martin and Connor with ease.

His father settled a straightforward look on him. "Things were different after you were born, Zach. Life has a way of changing things."

"As in?"

"We lost your brother." Simple words bearing grave intent. "Folks handle grief differently. Your mom felt guilty that Cam died, that she couldn't save him. It was no one's fault, we knew that, but sometimes..." He worked his jaw, remembering, then shrugged lightly. "Things eat at a person. When we had you, she stopped everything she was doing to take care of you, Ethan and Julia. The only thing she did on the side was raising puppies for folks. She didn't volunteer, didn't sing in the choir, didn't take food to the poor or help with Christmas baskets for needy families. All things she'd loved once. She cut out everything she used to do to put all of her efforts into being a mother."

"And you..."

"I let her do what she needed to do to help her through," Marty explained. "We'd seen marriages collapse after the loss of a child. I wasn't going to push her over some edge. So she took over with you guys and I ran the farm with hired help. One thing about running a farm." Marty turned his face toward the struggling field of corn to his right. "A farmer's got plenty of time to pray in the fields."

Marty hadn't abdicated his responsibilities because he loved farming more than his kids. He'd stepped aside to let Zach's mother assuage her guilt.

A thrust of shame knifed Zach.

He should have realized this before. Hearing his father's version softened childhood misconceptions. His mother's trips to the cemetery, the far-off expression she'd get now and then. Her dogged determination to see things through, guide her children.

As they pulled into Vince and Linda's driveway, Marty turned to Zach, full-face. "Here's the thing." He indicated Vince and Linda's place with a wave of his hand. "You came to Western New York to live independently a bunch of years back. I respect that."

"Command assigned me to Troop A. I said yes. They didn't give me a whole lot of say in the matter."

Marty grinned, understanding, but then he turned serious again. "If having us here crowds you too much, now's the time to say so. Before we climb out of this car and cut this deal."

His father was giving him a way out. Offering to give him space.

But he'd realized something these past weeks.

He liked family more than space.

He liked seeing his father's steady improvement now that the shock of waking up from his illness had worn off. Zach loved waking up to silly cartoons and Julia's boys having pillow fights in the family room, although he wished they'd stop hiding his TV remote.

He loved that he could be a help to his sister and a positive influence to her sons.

He climbed out of the car and jerked his head toward the house. "I've got all the space I need. Let's do this."

His father met his gaze, studied it, and then nodded, quick. "I'm all in."

CHAPTER FIFTEEN

THE REPORTER FROM THE *CLEARWATER Journal* snapped pictures of the farm and dairy store as Piper crossed the gravel drive. She paused, introduced herself and made small talk for a few minutes before turning on the recorder. Piper could only hope she didn't mess this meeting up, but the reporter stayed brief and to-the-point, letting Piper breathe easier. "Miss McKinney, do you find it ironic that the town is planning a year-long bicentennial celebration of Kirkwood Lake's roots while vying to take over one of its oldest farm properties?"

Piper didn't hesitate. "Of course I do. I represent the centennial farmers on the planning committee, which means Kirkwood Lake is home to generations of hardworking, industrious families. We'd like to keep that the norm."

"How do you plan to fight the town's move to obtain your lake frontage for the good of the community?"

"First, by pointing out that it isn't necessarily good for the community in the long run," Piper replied, "and second, by showing the town board that Kirkwood Lake is and always will be run by the people. Elected representatives are there to represent us. Not change things in spite of us."

The reporter smiled, thanked her and clicked off. She reached out a hand to shake Piper's. "My parents run a farm outside Cleveland. It's been tough to maintain things to keep the town happy, the neighbors happy and the livestock thriving. I think when my father throws in the towel, we'll be done, so I'm proud of you and the other farmers for standing up to this."

"Thank you."

Piper's phone rang again. Colin's number flashed. She took the call, waved goodbye to the reporter and moved to a quiet area near the barn. "Hello, Colin."

"You're really going to waste time and money fighting this, Piper? When you know it's the right thing to do? You'll lose land from Vince and Linda's place, you'll lessen the overall value of the farm by fighting the town on the lakeshore issue, and you'll waste valuable family money doing it. Why, Piper? Do you hate us that much?" Condescending anger edged each word, as if she were too stupid to see the writing on the wall.

She was done letting him berate her.

"I love the farm that much," she corrected him smoothly. "What does it matter to you when you get your share, Colin? Dad set the trust up so the farm would continue. You know that. He didn't want a historic farm to take another hit like it did when Mom walked out. He helped finance your education with a loan against this farm, remember? And then he did the same thing for Chas. Get a job, take care of your wife and celebrate the thought of a new child."

"It matters because we need the money now," Colin shot back. "Not in five years when you've run the place into the ground."

"You're jealous," Piper mused. "And yet, you hate the farm, so why would you be envious of it?"

"Ticked off, actually," Colin corrected her. "Because our happiness is directly tied to your ineptitude. And there's nothing we can do about it. That would make any man angry."

They could have worked harder. Joined her in the dream. Their dislike of the farm was probably the key to why Tucker set things up the way he did. Did their father realize how things would go?

Probably. But he trusted Piper to keep her chin up and her hands busy. "Colin, if I had liquid funds I'd buy you out right now, but I don't. So the monthly payments will have to suffice. Get a job."

He grumbled and hung up the phone.

"Ouch."

Piper turned at the sound of Rainey's voice. "And then some. Is that coffee?" She nodded to the to-go cup in Rainey's right hand.

"It is. I know you're heading back out, but I needed to ask you something."

Piper raised the cup. "You brought me coffee. Ask away."

"The kindergarten orientation is next Monday."

Piper nodded.

"Will you come with us? Me and the girls? I don't know them well enough yet, and I don't want to mess this up. And if I have to go away for a while again, I want to be sure everything's in order."

No matter what happened tomorrow night, Piper needed to reset her priorities. She'd known it for a while. Now she had to follow through, regardless. "I'll be there. And maybe we can take them out to lunch afterward. Make it a girl's day."

Rainey's smile told Piper she'd done the right thing. "I'd like that, Piper."

"Dad, are you going to the Braeburns' place with Piper and Berto tonight?" Zach asked

Marty nodded. "Figured I'd listen in. You want to ride along?"

"No." Zach grabbed his keys. "I've got to run to the barracks for an unscheduled meeting. Can you ride with Piper?"

"Yes. And I'm shopping for a truck this weekend. It's time to get my license renewed and get some wheels."

"Friday. With the boys. That will take their mind off Julia heading back to Ithaca without them."

His father laughed. "That will be a car-buying adventure to remember."

Zach pulled into the Zone 1 substation thirty minutes later. He met with a trio of supervisors and the county assistant district attorney. He laid out the facts as Piper told them, then left Rainey's fate in their hands.

On the way home, he prayed he'd done the right thing.

Piper, Lucia, Rainey and Berto arrived at the Town Hall thirty minutes early on Thursday night.

The grounds lay empty except for a bunch of kids playing basketball on the adjacent courts. Piper's hopes plummeted, until she got close to the building and read the flyers attached to the doors. She turned and waved for the others to stay in the car. "The meeting's been moved to the high school auditorium because of the large attendance."

She drove to the high school.

Cars overflowed the generous parking lot.

She parked on the street two blocks away and they walked to the meeting together, an unlikely looking family with ties that went thicker than blood—land ties, Tucker used to call them.

Folks streamed into the school from all sides. Some called greetings. Others didn't. But Piper estimated that three-quarters of the people were there to fight for farmers' rights. Ethan Harrison's advice rang in her ears.

Stop it now, before it gets to the courts. Once it's in the courts, it's out of your hands. Sage words from a farmer's son.

Marty Harrison gave Piper a crisp nod and wave from the back left-hand corner of the auditorium. She smiled and waved him over, but he shook his head, winked and smiled. In his left hand he held a folder of some sort. Maybe facts and figures from his farming days? Piper would welcome anything the expert dairyman could add to their cause.

Zach appeared at his father's side. They shared a few words, then he raised his gaze and spotted the McKinneys.

Zach's quick smile warmed her. His eyes held hope and promise, two things that seemed impossible a few short weeks ago.

But not anymore. Regardless of what happened tonight, the pledge in Zach's eyes and the strength of their faith would get them through. She knew it.

The large group was called to order by the town secretary. Minutes stretched as the board went through meeting protocol. When they finally opened the meeting to the long list of people who had signed up to offer opinions, Ron Palmeteer had the nerve to look patronizing and bored.

"You doing okay?" Zach crossed the room and crouched by her side. He reached over and covered her hands with his, then smiled right into her eyes. "You can do this."

"I can."

His smile widened. "Then go get 'em, tiger. They're calling your name."

Cheers erupted when Piper took the podium. She made her points in a clear, crisp voice, addressed the concerns of the town and followed with a farmer's point of view. "McKinney Farm isn't just a farm. It's a family heritage and a community legacy. It's a tradition. Farming is more than an enterprise in Kirkwood Lake. It's a way of life, a choice to remain rural and embrace our agricultural roots. Mr. Supervisor, when you first informed me of the town's interest in our waterfront, you used a quote from President Lincoln, how a house divided cannot stand."

Palmeteer nodded. He sent a quick gaze to her brothers, sitting on the far left.

"The actual origin of that quote is the Bible, sir. Lincoln was quoting the third chapter of Mark where he instructed people to form a unit and work together." She glanced around the room full of people. "I believe that's what you're witnessing here tonight. Our land values have escalated as the economy has improved." She let her gaze rest on the supervisor for long, pointed seconds. "But that elevated value will be reflected in tax hikes that may make living in Kirkwood Lake unaffordable for many. Like any responsible landowner, McKinney Farm will embrace a normal, gradual increase in land value but we will firmly oppose any political effort that artificially spikes land values to the detriment of the people."

Most of the crowd cheered. A few lakefront owners grumbled disagreement. Ron started to dismiss her address with a wave of his hand, but two of the board members began asking questions about land use and projections.

Their interrogation made the supervisor visibly nervous and more than a little angry, so when Marty Harrison approached the podium, Ron Palmeteer was already stressed.

"Mr. Supervisor and the board, I want to thank you for your attention to the wishes of your constituents tonight."

"And you are?"

"Martin Harrison. I live on Watkins Ridge with my son."

"Are you a Kirkwood Lake taxpayer, Mr. Harrison?"

Marty shifted an easy brow up. "I've paid my share over

the years, but not here as yet. But in an open forum, that shouldn't matter. What matters is what's fair and correct, regardless of whether I'm a landowner or a renter. Correct?"

A board member nodded. "Yes. Please continue."

Marty withdrew a sheet of paper from his folder. "This is a directive from New York State Agriculture and Markets that says a town in an agricultural district should do nothing to impede the acts pertaining to agriculture."

The supervisor's exasperated look said he knew all that and disagreed. "What you're missing is that the right of eminent domain prevails when the good of the larger community is involved. Surely you understand that roads must be built. Bridges reinforced. Libraries stocked and schools maintained. Infrastructure adjusted as benefits the needs of the majority."

Marty nodded. "Understood. And if the properties adjacent to the eminent domain then triple in value, that's not a bad thing for those particular property owners, is it?"

Ron squirmed because Marty was pointing out the benefits to the supervisor's private property behind Vince and Linda's farm.

Two more board members sat straighter, watching Marty and keeping an eye on the supervisor.

"However, if the land abutting Watkins Ridge above McKinney Farm is sold for farmland, this whole process becomes moot because there won't be any sprawling subdivision overlooking Kirkwood Lake on the upper west shore."

"Change can be hard, Mr. Harrison." The supervisor offered mock sympathy in a patronizing voice that infuriated Piper. Zach's hand on her arm kept her in her seat, but what she wanted to do was jump up and defend Marty's reputation by telling the room who he was and what he'd accomplished in Central New York.

Marty acknowledged the supervisor's words with a laugh. "Mr. Supervisor, you don't know the half of it." He sought out Zach in the crowd and smiled, because Marty understood change better than most now. "But it can also be beneficial." He waved another document for the board's attention. "I have here a bill of sale from Vince and Linda Hogan that names me the new owner of nearly ninety acres across from McKinney Farm."

Piper nearly choked. Marty bought Vince and Linda's land?

Zach's wink said he'd known about the deal and gave full approval.

"Which makes me a taxpayer, Mr. Supervisor."

Anger blotched Ron's complexion.

The board member to his left smiled. "Welcome to Kirkwood Lake, sir. Are you a farmer?"

"I am. I've also procured sixty acres from Wilma and Doug Johnson on the Upper Valley Road."

"Surrounding McKinney Farm."

"Proximity is a wonderful thing," Marty admitted with a grin. "My son lives here." He waved a hand toward Zach and the McKinney clan. "My daughter is moving here with my two grandsons. And I have a substantial nest egg at my disposal from the disbursement of my former farm, Tri-Central Dairy."

Gazes sharpened.

Tiny whispers danced across the room. Any farmer worth his salt held Tri-Central in high esteem. Having Marty Harrison's expertise in Kirkwood Lake would strengthen the farming core of the town.

And annoy the supervisor. Piper marked that a win-win.

"Mr. Harrison, let me be the first to welcome you to Kirkwood Lake." A board member broke protocol and circled the table to shake Marty's hand. "You've efficiently cut off any need we might have for a new sewer line stretching from the town to the proposed land north of McKinney Farm."

Marty nodded.

"And without a sewer line linking the town to developable land flanking the upper west shore, there's no reason to consider seizing anyone's land for eminent domain because the expected increase in population won't happen."

"My thoughts exactly." Marty shook the board member's hand and moved back to take a seat behind Piper.

The board moved for a dismissal.

Six voted "yes."

The lone dissenting vote was Ron Palmeteer.

The crowd erupted and it took nearly an hour of chatter and congratulations before Zach, Piper and the rest of the family made it to the parking lot.

Piper turned to face Marty once they were at Piper's car. "Thank you."

Marty grinned and hugged her. "The thanks is on my side, Piper. I woke up two months ago to circumstances that made me downright angry. Helping you on the farm made me see things through fresh eyes. And if my son is as smart as I think he is, we'll be looking at mutually beneficial contracting agreements in the future."

Zach's laughed and put his arm around Piper's shoulders.

"But in the meantime, I'd like to buy in as a partner to McKinney Farm," Marty continued. "That would give you the operating capital to move ahead with your breeding program and build the extra barn we'd need, plus you'd be able to buy out your brothers."

Buy out her brothers?

Piper shook her head. "Marty, that's too much. I appreciate what you're saying, but—"

"It's business, Piper." He didn't let her finish. "Ask my son, I'm pretty stuck-in-the-mud when it comes to business, and I never take an unnecessary risk. Slow and steady. That's the Harrison way."

"Except in certain matters," Zach's whisper tickled her ear. Sweet, wistful dreams of a true farm family danced in her mind, making her smile. "In those cases we Harrisons like to waste no time. So if we could make this all official and change your name to Harrison later this fall, I'd be okay with that. Gives us a long winter to plan." He looped his arms around her from the back and let his hands lay against her waist.

A home with Zach. Babies. A solid partnership with Marty, securing the farm financially.

Tears smarted Piper's eyes. Zach leaned in, saw the moisture and smiled, knowing. "Just say yes, honey. Keep it simple."

"Yes. To both of you. And tomorrow morning I'm going to give those two roosters all the extra feed they want, because we owe them. Big time."

Zach and Marty laughed together as the first drops of promised rain began to fall. "And *then* we cook 'em. Right?"

"We'll buy chicken at Tops Markets like everybody else," Piper scolded, but she laughed along with the men. "Leave my roosters alone."

"I will," Zach promised. He leaned in for a proper kiss as Marty moved off to the SUV. "You don't mind marrying a cop, Piper?"

Piper grinned and kissed him back, thoroughly. Convincingly. She ignored the rain, enjoying the cool feel of the moisture against her hair, her skin, safe in the circle of Zach's arms. "Not in the least," she whispered.

EPILOGUE

"I WILL NOT KNOW WHAT TO do with all this space when you are gone." Lucia's right hand fluttered slightly. Her deep breath said she would miss Piper's daily presence in the aging farmhouse.

But Piper merely laughed and grabbed her in a long hug. "I'll be right next door. After all this time, you're going to guilt-trip me for getting married?"

"I think it's the cleaning she's fretting over," Rainey announced as she stepped into the room. She waved her cell phone, impatient. "Our appointment at the bridal shop is in thirty minutes and it's a twenty-minute drive. Let's roll."

Lucia nodded. "Sonya? Dorrie? *Donde esta?*"

"We're here!" The twins raced across the hall, ponytails bouncing. Five-year-old excitement widened their eyes. "We really get to be flower girls, Aunt Piper? Both of us?"

"As if we could separate them," muttered Lucia.

Piper met Rainey's smile with a grin. "This could turn out to be a very short shopping trip." She angled a quick, knowing look at the girls. They loved to shop when it was all about them. Anything else taxed five-year-old impatience.

"Wrong." Rainey shooed the girls downstairs. "If they get a little crazy, Marty will take them off our hands so we can get things done. A fall wedding is lovely," she directed a pointed glance in Piper's direction, "unless it's nearly fall when you announce it."

Piper laughed, then shrugged. "Why wait? Small, sweet, and Reverend Smith said he'd do an outside ceremony at the lakeshore, weather permitting."

"The gazebo will be lovely," Lucia declared. "White lights, white netting…"

"And those lit-up Mason jars hanging everywhere," Rainey added.

"Flowers."

"And fall foliage. So many colors."

"*Tan perfecto!*" Lucia's tone underscored her approval.

"Piper?" Zach's deep voice called from downstairs, a voice that beckoned the womanly spirit within her.

"Coming." Piper hurried downstairs and straight into Zach's waiting arms. He kissed her good-morning, a kiss that made her long to hurry the weeks away. But Lucia was already prepared to do her bodily harm for planning a wedding in the middle of harvest, so she'd keep her wishes to herself.

"When will you be back?" He whispered the words into her ear, his tone reflecting her emotions. Being separated for hours was too much for them these days.

She leaned back against his steady, strong arms, knowing they'd hold her. "Probably not before you go to work."

"Wrong answer." He fake-scowled, then pulled her close for drawn-out seconds. "Then I will come for you in the morning. We'll go to church together and then crunch numbers."

"Numbers." She nodded, firm, as if she had a clue what he was talking about. "Sure. Cows? Heifers? Corn yields?"

"Babies."

Her heart melted at the sweet, husky sound of his voice near her ear. "You mean how many?"

"Yes. That's a four-bedroom house over there." He eyed the west-facing window. "And farm help is at a premium these days, therefore the sooner the better, right?"

She batted his arm, returned his fake scowl with a slightly more real one, then smiled. "We'll talk. Then leave it to God."

His smile said he wouldn't disagree. He took a broad but reluctant step back. "You've got money for your dress?"

"Thanks to your father's partnership, my wedding budget isn't nearly as tight as it would have been."

"And the goat is her dowry. Lucky you." Rainey made the remark as she prodded her mother down the stairs. "Your hair is fine, we're late, let's go."

Zach reached out a hand to pause Rainey's progress as she drew near. She stopped, surprised, then took the envelope he'd extended her way. "What's this?"

"Read it and see."

Puzzled, her brows knit as she opened the envelope. Then she sat, stunned, tears running down her cheeks.

"Rainey. What is it? What's wrong?" Piper sank into the chair alongside her, grabbed Rainey's hand, then turned and scolded Zach. "What have you done? Why is she crying?"

"She's happy, would be my guess."

"Happy?"

"Yes." Rainey reached out and clutched Zach's hand. "You did this."

"I went to some very important people and told the truth. And then I prayed, loud and long. The rest was up to them."

"Larraina? What is wrong?" Lucia's face showed motherly concern as she hurried back to them.

"Nothing, Mama. Nothing at all." She waved the paper. "I'm free."

"You are…?" Confusion marred Lucia's features. "I do not understand."

"Rainey will not have to face consequences for breaking her parole. The assistant district attorney and the judge decided that her assistance in putting away a large-scale racketeering ring outweighed her youthful indiscretion. And while they were at it, they reopened the case of the convenience store robbery and have arrested Chloe Markakis in California. With the current evidence supporting Rainey's story, her record will be expunged."

"Cleared?" Piper grabbed him around the neck and hugged him. "You think she'll be cleared, Zach?"

"I know she will. Because in the end, the truth will set you free."

Rainey stood. She hugged him, swiped her eyes, hugged her mother and then tapped her watch. "I am overwhelmed. And so grateful. But if we're late to this appointment, you might be getting married in blue jeans."

"I wouldn't care," Zach declared, grinning.

"But I would." Lucia's scowl said only a white dress would do, and no one messed with Lucia's scowl. Ever. "You." She reached up and took Zach's face between two strong, brown hands and then pulled him down to kiss his cheek. "You honor us by being part of this family, Zach Harrison. I will be pleased to call you my son."

Zach's gaze softened and he surprised Lucia by giving her a big, old-fashioned hug. "Thank you."

The sound of joyous chatter trailed as Rainey and Lucia hurried to the car. Zach gave Piper one last kiss. "Have fun. I miss you already."

"Me, too." His words blessed her as she returned his hug, then hustled to the waiting car.

She began the summer in prayer, the future dim, her prospects unwieldy on multiple levels.

Now the future lay open to a world of happiness.

She'd started the summer with intercessions, asking God's help.

She'd end it with gentle thanksgiving in the arms of the man she loved. As they pulled away, she saw Marty approach Zach from across the yard. Martin and Connor were walking the pup they'd decided to keep on one leash and Beansy on another.

The pup was less than cooperative as his tiny legs got tangled in the leash.

The goat didn't appear to be any happier.

Zach picked up the pup, saving him from further childish intervention. Marty followed suit with the goat, two big men, sheltering God's creatures from busy boy hands.

It was a Norman Rockwell picture in the making. Two men, faith-filled, believing that hard work could prevail. Believing in her.

That was reason enough to smile right there.

DEAR READER,
Farmer Dave and I own a farm in Western New York. It was actually "McKinney Farm" in 1854, bought by the McKinney family, early settlers in our town.

It's not huge… fifty acres. Only about 35 are "tillable", able to be used for crops, but as our retirement project we started a pumpkin farm! Up until 2014, we rented out the land to others and then we got the brilliant (Dave says that descriptor is up for debate!) idea to work the farm ourselves… and what began as somewhat tedious vegetable growing is now an amazingly fun and popular fall farm with all the fun, décor and beauty a northern fall entails. We are having such a good time and people love coming to see the farm in its autumn glory of over seventy different kinds of pumpkins and squashes, cornstalks, hay bales, gift shop, baked goods, miniature donkeys, a kids' playground, and two acres of gorgeous displays. We are so blessed.

I love farm country. Small towns, rolling hills or long, flat expanses, I love living in the country. I'm also blessed to live near beautiful lakes, and how fun it is to create a new rural and riparian community in Kirkwood Lake (based on Chautauqua Lake, NY).

I've watched multiple family farms disappear over the last fifteen years. I've seen homes sold, and brothers and sisters estranged. The legal process for entrusting a farm is tricky. Most parents think their children will rise to the occasion and work things out, but that doesn't always happen when money is involved. Using Marty's and Piper's farms as examples, I've tried to show how difficult it can be for the current generation to keep the family farm afloat. Like Shammah in the book of Samuel, Piper fights the good fight, often feeling alone in her uphill struggle.

We buy local whenever possible. We would rather pay the local farmer directly as often as we can but that's growing more difficult each year.

We support our town's goal to maintain an agricultural community. And when folks move to a farming community, they should be prepared to accept all the nuances of country living, not just the pretty landscape outside their windows. Including roosters, of course!

I hope you enjoyed this story of a new beginning and that you'll come back and visit Kirkwood Lake often. As always, please come visit me at my website ruthloganherne.com and www.ruthysplace.com, friend me on Facebook, email me at loganherne@gmail.com.

I love hearing from you!

May God bless you in abundance,

ABOUT THE AUTHOR

MULTI-PUBLISHED, BESTSELLING inspirational author Ruth Logan Herne is the kind of gal you want to share a cuppa with or even a box of cookies. Ruthy has had over seventy novels and novellas published through multiple publishers and independent works, including dozens of Love Inspired books, Guideposts, Inc. mysteries, cowboy stories, historicals and her crazy popular "Wishing Bridge" series, available through Amazon. She and her husband "Farmer Dave" own a rapidly growing pumpkin farm in Hilton, NY. What began as a family project has become an amazingly busy enterprise, but that's the fun of a big family. There are lots of helping hands on board! She loves God, her family, being part of a great small town and laughing with children of every age. You can find Ruthy on Facebook, visit her website ruthloganherne.com or email her at loganherne@gmail.com.

KIRKWOOD LAKE RECIPE CORNER

Lucia McKinney's Tres Leches Cake
(Three–Milk Cake)

SPONGE CAKE:

1 cup all purpose flour
6 eggs (3 will be separated, but not permanently! No lawyers needed!)
1 cup sugar
2 teaspoons almond flavoring, if desired. (We love almond sponge so we add it.)

2 large mixing bowls

In one bowl, put three eggs and 3 egg yolks. Add the sugar and beat with mixer until pale yellow in color. This may take several minutes. In second bowl (making sure there's no grease on/in bowl) beat the 3 egg whites until stiff peaks form. Fold the whipped egg whites into the beaten egg/sugar mixture. Sift the 1 cup of flour over the mix and fold in with spatula, just until flour streaks disappear. Don't overmix... We want the cake spongy and light, ready to receive the milk syrup later... Oh, yum....

Using spatula, gently put cake batter into buttered 13" x 9" pan.

Bake at 325° on center rack until cake is puffed and golden. Sides should pull away from pan slightly. Once cake is removed from oven, allow to cool a few minutes, then flip cake onto large tray or plate with sides to prevent sauce from spilling over. Using a large fork or a steel knife sharpener (this is what I prefer, those rounded steel rods that come with knife sets… perfect for poking holes!) poke holes at ½" intervals throughout cake. No, you don't need to measure the distance… "guesstimate", okay? Nothing goes wrong if holes are closer… you want that milk sauce to penetrate throughout the cake.

MILK SAUCE:

Mix together in medium saucepan:
½ cup corn syrup
¾ cup evaporated milk
¾ cup sugar

Heat to boiling over medium heat, and then simmer about five minutes, until pale caramel/gold in color.

Mix in:
1 12 oz. can evaporated milk
2/3 cup coconut milk (for coconut variety) or 2/3 cup half-and-half or light cream
Mix together, then spoon over cake slowly, allowing syrup to drench cake.

1 can sweetened condensed milk can be used instead

of first three ingredients, but if you don't have it on hand, the mix of sugar, corn syrup and evaporated milk makes an amazing milk sauce and only takes minutes on top of the stove. It does bubble, so make sure pan is big enough so you don't overflow. If using the canned variety, no need to heat.

Refrigerate cake, then top with *WHIPPED CREAM*:

Whip 2 cups heavy whipping cream and ½ cup sugar until stiff peaks form. Spread over cooled cake. May be garnished with fruit, nuts, coconut, etc. Whatever you like! This great recipe has become a family favorite for the Blodgett family here at Blodgett Family Farm— and now the McKinney's of Kirkwood Lake!

ALSO BY RUTH LOGAN HERNE

If you enjoyed Zach and Piper's story, here's a list of other books by bestselling author Ruth Logan Herne:

Ruthy's Amazon Author page and books:
http://amzn.to/1v26FHw
★ ★ ★
INDEPENDENTLY PUBLISHED BOOKS:
Running on Empty
Try, Try Again
Safely Home
Refuge of the Heart
More Than a Promise
The First Gift
From This Day Forward
Christmas on the Frontier
The Sewing Sisters' Society
A Most Inconvenient Love
★ ★ ★
NORTH COUNTRY SERIES
Waiting Out the Storm
Season of Hope
Winter's End
★ ★ ★
SOUTHERN TIER ROMANCE
Reunited Hearts
Small Town Hearts
A Family to Cherish
The Lawman's Second Chance
★ ★ ★

FROM WATERFALL PRESS/AMAZON/
INDEPENDENT
Welcome to Wishing Bridge
At Home in Wishing Bridge
Finding Peace in Wishing Bridge
Embracing Light in Wishing Bridge
Reclaiming Hope in Wishing Bridge
Kindling Christmas in Wishing Bridge
★ ★ ★
FROM WATERBROOK PRESS/PENGUIN/
RANDOM HOUSE
Back in the Saddle
Home on the Range
Peace in the Valley
★ ★ ★
LOVE INSPIRED BOOKS
Mended Hearts
Yuletide Hearts
His Mistletoe Family
★ ★ ★
KIRKWOOD LAKE SERIES
Falling for the Lawman
The Lawman's Holiday Wish
Loving the Lawman
Her Holiday Family
Healing the Lawman's Heart
★ ★ ★
GRACE HAVEN SERIES
An Unexpected Groom
Her Unexpected Family
Their Surprise Daddy
The Lawman's Yuletide Baby
Her Secret Daughter
★ ★ ★
SHEPHERD'S CROSSING SERIES
Her Cowboy Reunion

A Cowboy Christmas (with Linda Goodnight)
A Cowboy in Shepherd's Crossing
Healing the Cowboy's Heart
★ ★ ★
GOLDEN GROVE SERIES
A Hopeful Harvest
Learning to Trust
Finding Her Christmas Family
★ ★ ★
KENDRICK CREEK SERIES
Rebuilding Her Life
The Path Not Taken
A Foster Mother's Promise
★ ★ ★
FROM BIG SKY CONTINUITY/LOVE INSPIRED
BOOKS:
His Montana Sweetheart

★ ★ ★
FROM SUMMERSIDE PRESS:
Love Finds You in the City at Christmas
★ ★ ★
From Barbour Publishing:
Homestead Brides Collection
★ ★ ★
FROM ZONDERVAN/HARPER COLLINS
All Dressed Up in Love
★ ★ ★
CONTRIBUTING AUTHOR
"MYSTERIES OF MARTHA'S VINEYARD"
Available at Guideposts.com

A Light in the Darkness
Swept Away
Catch of the Day
Just over the Horizon

★ ★ ★

CONTRIBUTING AUTHOR
"SAVANNAH SECRETS" MYSTERY SERIES
Available at Guideposts.com

A Fallen Petal
Patterns of Deception
Jingle Bell Heist
★ ★ ★

CONTRIBUTING AUTHOR
"MIRACLES AND MYSTERIES OF MERCY
HOSPITAL" SERIES:
Prescription for Mystery
Merciful Secrecy
★ ★ ★

FROM GUIDEPOSTS' "LOVE'S A MYSTERY"
SERIES:
Love's a Mystery in Sleepy Hollow, NY
Love's a Mystery in Cut and Shoot, Texas
★ ★ ★

FROM GUIDEPOSTS' "WHISTLE STOP CAFÉ
MYSTERIES" SERIES:
As Time Goes By
That's My Baby